PHOEBE'S KNEE

Other books by B. Comfort available from
Foul Play Press

The Cashmere Kid
Grave Consequences

B. COMFORT

PHOEBE'S KNEE

A Tish McWhinny Mystery

A Foul Play Press Book

The Countryman Press
Woodstock, Vermont

1

I opened my eyes slowly, wakened by cool fingers on my wrist. The nurse, silhouetted by the window, studied her watch. Chinese, I guessed. Her long black hair was arranged in a chignon. Her dainty nose barely held up her half glasses.

"Am I in China?"

My last memory was of losing my balance and crashing painfully into a chasm or dark hole. The possibility that I had tumbled on through to China seemed reasonable.

"You're awake." The nurse patted the back of my hand. "Do you know your name?"

"Letitia McWhinny, but am I in China?"

"What month is it?"

"August. Am I . . ."

"How old are you?" The nurse persisted with her questions.

Patience isn't my long suit. "Sixty-five" sounded more like a snarl than a number. "For heaven's sake, where am I?"

"The Putnam Memorial Hospital in Bennington, Vermont."

I thought about that a minute. "How did I get here?"

"The rescue squad brought you."

Trying to follow the course of events, I faded from the world of transportation and geography.

The next time I opened my eyes it was in response to having my eyelids pried up by a fair-haired youngster. He examined my eyeballs with a flashlight.

"I'm Dr. Williams. You sustained a heavy blow, Mrs. . . . "—he looked at the chart—"McWhinny, but you've got a tough skull." It didn't feel tough. "You'll be okay. You've got a couple of cracked ribs. Nothing we can do about them. Just don't laugh."

I wasn't about to laugh. My neck and head hurt so much I wanted to cry.

"Here's your husband." Dr. Williams ushered in Hilary Oats, who wasn't my husband. Doug died eight years ago. Hilary was a neighbor from Lofton, my drinking companion and alternative to frozen dinners. Hilary liked to straddle chairs, but the shape of this one defeated him. He pushed it aside and bent over to look at me.

"What in hell have you been doing?" Hilary looked like Shakespeare except that his beard was square, not pointed. I hoped his gruff question masked tenderer feelings. He sounded as though I'd done something deliberately to annoy him.

"I fell into a hole."

"Probably a root cellar."

"I hope the young reporter is all right."

"Reporter? I don't know what you're talking about."

Suddenly I was frightened. "Hilary," I must have shouted. "Lulu, where's Lulu?"

"Calm down, Tish. I've got her." He held my wrists as I tried frantically to get out of bed.

"I left Lulu at my house curled up on the couch

2

listening to the Emerson Quartet." Hilary was referring to my dog. "They say you'd be gathering moss in that old root cellar if Lulu hadn't acted like Lassie and Rin Tin Tin rolled into one."

"But the reporter, where is he?"

Hilary shrugged. "Don't know what you're talking about."

In response to my questions, Hilary explained that upon returning from Manchester he had stopped at the Lofton post office and there was Herb, our postmaster, with his arm around Lulu, my pug, who was sitting on the counter as though posing for a postage stamp. Herb told him that a couple of men rebuilding the Lawtons' back wall had heard Lulu barking as she ran towards them, then ran out of sight, barking. They finally caught on and followed her to the opening of a root cellar. They found me lying inside, unconscious. One of them ran back and called the rescue squad. They brought Lulu to the post office.

"But where's the reporter?" I tried to sit up again. Stilettos jabbed my lungs. The pain was so fierce I could hardly speak. That nice young man with the camera, the reporter. I remember clutching him as the rocks gave way under me. He must be hurt.

"This reporter you say was with you. Maybe he went off to report that you fell in a hole and the stone masons got to you first. Don't suppose he'd just leave you there."

"Of course he wouldn't."

"Maybe," Hilary said beaming, "he pushed you in the hole. Maybe he wanted to be alone with Lulu."

I guess Hilary thought he was being funny, but while he was still talking, I succumbed to whatever dope the nurse had put in the I.V. I slipped away to sounds of malevolent whispering and spooky images

3

of hooded men in long robes. Probably I dreamt about the cult that had moved into Lofton this summer. They called themselves The Ring of Right, and were instantly dubbed the Ringers.

It was Lulu who had cocked her head that fateful morning, then barked at the young man who emerged from a dusty Volvo. He stretched his lanky body and tossed a road map through the car window.

Seated in the shade created by the Lofton general store, I had the pleasure of examining the stranger unobserved. I consider staring a painter's prerogative.

A hiker perhaps, attracted by Lofty's many ski trails now blazing with wildflowers. Straps that crisscrossed his chest were fastened to a camera and an equipment case. Businesslike, I thought, but not seriously professional. His slim hips barely held up khaki cutoffs. Skinny was an accurate description, though his conformation suggested an athlete. His red rugby shirt looked expensive. I wondered if his sneakers would make it through the day. Scratching his fair hair with the eraser end of a pencil, the young man screwed up his features into a picture of perplexity.

Something about him made me smile. I wondered what this engaging wanderer was doing in Lofton. I decided that after graduating from college he had decided to tour New England with his camera, a last fling before starting a job. Where? I dismissed a bank and I couldn't see him behind a desk. Maybe he was here to apply for a job with the forest service or perhaps at the ski area. I'd heard they were recruiting young talent for their expansion programs. I did peg him as an outdoor type, but the round wire-rimmed glasses and the briefcase could indicate some quiet pursuit.

While I was still making up my mind about the young stranger's future employment, he walked towards the store and with a pleasant smile sat down on the bench beside us.

"A pug," he said, patting Lulu. "Love 'em. My grandmother had one. Her pug's name was Phoebe."

"Anyone who had a grandmother who had a pug called Phoebe is highly acceptable to Lulu and me." I introduced myself. Lew Weber was his name.

"Wish he was a bloodhound."

"She," I corrected.

"Wish she was a bloodhound." By then Lulu was arranging herself on his lap. His long bare legs made it a tricky operation.

"A bloodhound?" I asked.

"Yeah. You wouldn't know where I can find those cult types that have moved in, would you?"

Unlike this young man, most strangers assumed I knew everything because I looked like a wise old owl. My mop of frizzy hair and huge horned-rim glasses (trifocals) gave a false impression of wisdom and omnipotence.

"They said," he continued, "the place they lived was on Main Street."

He stood up with Lulu tucked under his arm. "I love this town. Grandma Moses, where are you?" Lew pointed towards the Town Hall. "Nifty sign."

Looking in one direction down Main Street you could see the Methodist church with its new coat of white paint. Beyond it the Antique Barn and next the O'Hara house, painted a slightly rancid yellow. In the other direction there was Pete's garage, which had been built onto the front of his fine Federal house. Four more white houses and then the Town Hall.

Last month, a committee of two had whitewashed the tiny brick building and by request I had fabricated a plywood sign for over the doorway cut out in the shape of Lofty Mountain. I had painted it green and glued raised letters in white across the bottom spelling "Lofton Village, Vermont." Someone asked me when they were going to attach the basketball hoop, but most people thought it was great.

The post office and half a dozen more white houses made up the rest of Main Street. I was pleased by the young stranger's reaction to my sign.

"I've always wanted to come back to Lofton."

"Back?"

"We came here as kids once for a couple of days with our grandmother."

"And you don't remember Amber Trees, the big house beyond the gates?"

"Not really. My brother and I spent every waking moment in the woods. We were explorers. I remember we wore knapsacks full of emergency supplies. Peanut butter sandwiches, Oreos, a compass, of course. Teddy insisted on taking beads to trade with the Indians. Grandma always made us take a tiny alarm clock. We had to head for the inn when it rang. It was the first place I ever had French toast. It made Teddy gag."

Lew sat with Lulu facing him. "They look like bats with their ears up." He held her silky ears away from her head. "At least we thought Phoebe did, but she was a black pug."

"When were you here, nineteen years ago?"

He nodded. "Twenty."

"Amber Trees was still occupied by the original owners," I said. "Then for a couple of years it served as a nursing home. Now the Ringers."

"'The Ringers'?" That's what they call them?"

I explained the derivation of the name while he took out a red kerchief and cleaned his glasses and dusted off his camera case.

"I think I can cope with them," he said confidently. "I'm doing a piece for Vermont Valley Monthly. They want the lowdown on some of the sects and cults that have been cropping up around the state. Lofton is my first stop."

"What's the purpose of this cult," he wanted to know. "What do they do?"

"Nobody actually knows yet. They just started moving in last month. They claim to be agrarians. Presumably, they intend to make their living from the earth. "Quite a trick in Vermont." Harmless, according to the real estate agent, Scarlett O'Hara, who had sold them altogether too much of Lofton. Harmless farmers, she had said, with some common belief. But I wondered. "The rumors, of course, are wild."

"Wild? Like what?"

"One, that their garments have no pockets because they think pockets harbor evil spirits. Two, they worship pigs. I like that one, but my favorite is that each Ringer has to have an enema every day. In my opinion, that last entry accounts for their dreary demeanor." Lew laughed. "And no electric lights. I'm told they like to do whatever they do in the dark."

"Considering their practices," Lew said, "I hope they approve of plumbing."

I touched his camera and shook my head. "Better not—they're camera shy."

The truth was I didn't give a damn about the Ringers. I'd heard nothing but Ringer talk for two months and I was sick to death of the subject. But Lew encouraged me to tell him more.

I told him Alan Smith was the unlikely name of their leader. He was referred to by his disciples as The Marshal. But it was Alan Smith's name that was affixed to legal papers for the acquisition of Amber Trees and the Valley Farms.

"Thank God he isn't a developer," our postmaster had said. But most Loftonites weren't that sanguine. Was it better to have condos full of skiers and vacationers and second homes dotting the landscape, or an ever expanding band of cultists with God knows what objectives in mind?

Vermont was not a new host to cults. Last summer, the papers were full of the appalling treatment of children by members of the Northeast Kingdom Community Church up near the Canadian border. Here there were no children, which seemed odd given all the talk of rampant sex and ancient pagan rites.

Hilary called the head guru, The Marshal, the dreary druid. Big deal, he said, being head honcho of a bunch of beats in sackcloth and sandals. Another neighbor called them the born-again flakies.

The town zoning board had been persuaded that Smith and his disciples simply wanted to live in peace and raise their own food. They applied to the board for a permit to build a couple of greenhouses, and convinced them that they would be innocuous neighbors.

Strenuous objections were raised by many residents, but the deeds were signed without much fuss. It wasn't until the Ringers started to move in that the Lofton Corporation, which ran the ski area and other mountain attractions, became concerned. They were aghast when they realized this unsmiling drab mob of strangers would quickly cast a pall over Lofton's cheerful picture postcard image. Too late.

The zoning board granted the Ringers permission to put up fences wherever they chose as long as any such fences were not visible from the road. Truckloads of chain link fence arrived in town, but nobody seemed to know just where they were installed. There was a precedent for fences. Solzhenitsyn was protected by a chain link fence where he lived, not far from Lofton, but most Vermonters regarded a fence as an arrangement for keeping livestock enclosed, not to keep people out.

Someone had seen a greenhouse being assembled and was relieved to see that they were made of plastic sheeting stretched over a frame, possibly because it made their invasion seem less permanent. But who would have paid three-quarters of a million for Amber Trees and the farm properties without a serious permanent intention?

"I think," Lew said, "your zoning board may have made a serious mistake."

When Lew asked me if I could show him where to get the best pictures of the Ringers' house, of course I jumped at the chance.

That's how Lew Weber and Lulu and I happened to fall into this hole together.

We walked along our well-tended dirt and gravel main street. Lew observed that in most places dirt roads were losing the battle to asphalt and tar. I told him that we fought hard to keep our old-fashioned ochre roads. Every year at town meeting the same group voted for hard-topping. Too much dust, they complained. So far, the vociferous majority had won.

Lew Weber satisfied my curiosity by telling me that after college he'd spent a year working for the New

York Post but had always wanted to live in Vermont and start his own paper. He was trying to get a little more experience before taking the plunge.

He wasn't the first person to take a picture of the Lofton Inn. Its inviting facade appeared in many pamphlets and magazines extolling Vermont's charm. Eclectic New England was how Hilary described its architectural style. I loved the glass panels on either side of the entrance and the long windows across the front of the building.

Just beyond the Inn was the stone wall and entrance gate to Amber Trees. Looking through the gate we could just make out the newly erected wire fence. On the other side of the fence a female Ringer was standing on her head.

I heard the click of Lew's shutter before I could stop him, but nothing happened. No guard leapt out at us, and the woman remained serenely balanced on her natural tripod of head and elbows.

"Let's not push our luck, Lew." I urged him up the street with the promise of a splendid camera site on a hill behind the Ringers' barn.

My white house with its Federal serenity was nicely related to the other houses on Main Street—that is, until you walked around the back and saw the modern studio I had built. After Doug died, I had decided to become a year-rounder.

We walked across the clearing behind my studio and hiked up a rocky hill.

"Just exactly where is your boundary and how much of the land do you own behind the cult house?"

"Their land goes up the mountain till it joins the national forest. Mine joins the forest too, you'll see."

Lew waved his arm to the right. "Would you say they owned all this?"

10

"I daresay, but the best way to find out is to ask our town clerk. That is, if you can find her. There's a big chart on the wall that will answer your questions."

I told him about the rolls of cyclone fencing. "I haven't walked up Lofty lately. I don't know what the so-and-so's have been doing."

Lew rubbed his angular jaw. "Suppose I wanted to camp up in the woods on your property. Would that be okay?"

"Sure, I don't know why not. And if you don't build a fire you can camp in the National Forest."

Walking down the other side of the hill it happened. We were engaged in companionable conversation when suddenly the earth collapsed underneath my feet. I reached out for Lew, who was in front of me, but he slipped out of my grasp. I must have thrown my arms up in the air because my chest seemed to explode. I heard but didn't feel the crack on my head. All I can remember thinking is, oh dear, my glasses.

My brief stay in the hospital was almost pleasant, thanks to my nurse. She tied a knot in a plastic bag. "I put your film in here along with a couple of other things that were in your pockets."

Film? What was she talking about? I used film for work only and didn't have my camera when I fell in the dungeon.

"It has to be yours, Mrs. McWhinny. You'll see when you have it developed."

I realized instantly that the film must belong to Lew Weber. The nurse waved a red kerchief that I recognized as Lew's. "I'll put this back in your pocket."

There were quite a few things to be investigated when I got home.

"First," I told Hilary as we left Bennington and drove north towards Manchester, "I want to find out what happened to that young reporter." I waved the bag with the film in front of his eyes. "This film has got to belong to Lew. Wonder what's on it. Let's stop at the camera store. We'll have it back by tomorrow."

Hilary made a sensible suggestion. "Maybe you should wait. This fellow may not want to have you fooling with his film. The pictures may not be particularly illuminating," he added. "Probably a roll of pictures of a birthday party at the Brattleboro Retreat."

We occasionally reflected on whether our futures might be entwined with the Retreat. Hilary, ten years older than I am, was sure that at any given moment he'd land there in a straitjacket. I had promised to keep him company.

"And second, Hilary," I said, "what's with this root cellar? You've lived here most of your life. Ever heard of anyone falling into a root cellar or, for that matter, who needs a root cellar? In Vermont? Don't you store stuff under the barn or in any old cellar?" I challenged him: "Name me one person with a root cellar."

Hilary gave up. I waited in the car while he went in to fetch Lulu. What a kind friend he was. I mustn't, I reminded myself, take him for granted. The hills were swarming with unattached women eager to devour Hilary. Distinguished looking, witty and frequently wise, he was considered a catch. Some of the predators had serious intentions, but most wanted an escort, dinner partner and playmate. Hilary confided to me last week that a woman I knew quite well had tried to persuade him to join her on a trip around the world, all expense paid. He refused. Had he looked a bit smug just lately or was it bemused?

12

Hilary had sold his bindery in Rutland a few years ago, and announced he intended to spend the rest of this life reading, cooking and playing Scrabble with me.

Adjusting the rear view mirror, I examined my face. A lifetime of squinting at tennis balls, beach-combing and painting landscapes in the noonday sun had taken their toll. My elastic face was a faithful register of my emotions, which added daily to my collection of wrinkles and lines. Kay said my face looked well lived in. When Hilary wanted to butter me up, he insisted that with a hat on I looked just like Katherine Hepburn, a resemblance unremarked by others.

Lulu nearly killed me with her enthusiastic greeting. "Please take me to the store, Hil. I must find out if anyone saw the reporter. Maybe he left a message."

Hilary emerged from the store shaking his head. "No one knows anything about him. Never saw him. Didn't see him here with you before you took off. They wanted to know all about you. Marge says she'll be up to see you later—I gather bringing food."

2

There was a skylight in my bathroom. I watched blue sky turn to gray and then become a panel of starless indigo. Every so often I twisted the old-fashioned spigot which spelled HOT. I soaked and pondered.

My initial anger at Lew Weber for his callous and thoughtless departure was fading. I felt certain he was a decent person and probably incapable of abandoning an unconscious old lady in a hole or a ditch or whatever it was. What could have happened to him? His car had been parked between the store and the post office clearly visible from both places, but neither the Macys nor Herb remembered seeing it at any time. I planned to call the rescue squad first to thank them, then to ask if they had noticed anything about the root cellar—blood perhaps? The uneasy thought made me suddenly feel trapped in the tub.

I didn't feel up to tackling the enormous roast beef sandwich Marge Macy had left for me. I didn't even want a drink. A rubdown with Tiger Balm helped and a pill the doctor had given me finished me off for the night.

As I was feeding Lulu the next morning, Kay Anderson, owner of the Green Mountain Gallery, called from Manchester, to scold me, I was sure, for not bringing her the clipping for a brochure for my next exhibition. She wanted to send the material to the printers.

When Kay started her gallery in Manchester a few years ago, she latched on to me. I don't know whether she thought my portraits were marvelous or whether I was a good meal ticket. I had to plead for mercy. Kay made me work like a serf. But I loved it. She sparkled with vitality and made me feel like a combination of Mary Cassatt and Georgia O'Keefe, with a little Rosa Bonheur thrown in. She sold everything I painted at astronomical prices and kept finding ghastly looking people, and altogether too many children, for portrait commissions.

"How are you, Tish? I've heard all about it. How in the world did that photographer happen to hit you on the head with a rock?"

"Typical grapevine report!" I described what had happened yesterday. My ribs hurt so much I started sniveling. Kay made me promise not to move a muscle—she'd be in Lofton in fifteen minutes. Then, she said, between us we'd figure out what had happened to Lew Weber. I could imagine her eyes getting even greener at the thought of tracking a missing man. I looked at my watch. Aside from what I hoped was a genuine fondness for me, Kay needed no urging to come to Lofton. At the slightest excuse she raced over the mountain because she had a crush on Terry Fink, one of the new owners of the Lofton Inn. Usually the situation was reversed. Kay was pursued by armies of men. It made me laugh to see her dithering around about Terry. I had a feeling it was hopeless.

My next phone call wasn't as pleasant. A nasal sexless voice inquired, "Mrs. McWhinny?"

"This is she."

"The roll of film you took from the cave yesterday.

15

It belongs to us. Put it on the porch and someone will pick it up right away."

I nearly exploded. "And just who the hell do you think you are?"

I didn't permit a reply. Lying, I added, "I don't know what you're talking about." Lulu jumped off my lap with alarm when I roared, "What a nerve!" and slammed down the receiver, causing the film to fall off the table and roll across the floor.

I was still trembling when Kay ran through the door and hugged me. I had told her about my head but not my cracked ribs and nearly fainted in her exuberant embrace. She rushed into the kitchen and came back with a bottle of household ammonia and stuck it under my nose. Once again I nearly passed out. I waved Kay away and leaned my head back on Aunt Mable's antimacassar.

Kay retrieved the plastic container of film and held it while I told her about the phone call. She opened the screen door and looked up and down the street.

"Come on, Tish, let's get out of here."

"Now wait," I protested.

"Let's take the film to Rutland. There's a guy who will develop it in less than an hour."

"We should give this some thought, Kay. Maybe take it to the police or send it to his newspaper." She swept away my doubts.

"Come on, Tish, no time to lose. Let's avoid the creep who called you."

I picked up my wallet, some dark glasses and put on Lulu's leash. "This may not be wise, Kay."

"I think it's wise," she said. "I just hope it's safe."

Crawling into her low sports car was agony. We didn't see a soul as Kay maneuvered the car around a couple of sleeping dogs and whipped up a cloud of

16

dust as we catapulted towards route 11. In Rutland, Kay left me parked by the curb and she went to deliver the film and do some errands.

I watched the population paw through racks of clothing arranged along Main Street. We had hit the city in time for the late summer sidewalk sale. It was depressing. The hopeless expression of the faces of the would-be buyers told me that they knew what I knew, which was that all the garments would be size 4 or 22, belts 18 inches or less and slippers made for midgets. Only the rack outside the bookstore tempted me, but I was too tired and tender to move. Thinking about Lew my forehead felt as furrowed as Lulu's. Kay returned with an ice cream cone for me holding high the envelope of photographs. Speedy Photo had produced them in record time and, once behind the wheel, Kay quickly flipped through the first few snapshots and handed them to me with a groan.

Hilary was right. I don't know what I had expected. What I saw were pictures of an old man grinning in front of a horseshoe arch of flowers with a banner that offered greetings to Harry on his one hundredth birthday. Kay handed me a handful more of people shaking Harry's hand. I wanted to weep.

"Look at this, Tish."

At first I was puzzled. Marks drawn in the sand with a child's finger? Not sand, of course. Markings on rock. They looked like Roman numerals. Three or four pictures were quite similar. The marks were slightly different.

"These must have been taken inside the root cellar, Tish. What does it mean? That guy, the reporter, must have thought they were important."

"So did the person who called me."

17

"Hey, look at this." The last picture Kay handed me was different. In the lower right corner a dark object appeared, a half oval, and the upper third of the picture was a lighter color. It looked as though Lew had held his hand over a corner of the lens.

Tapping the picture on my chin, I gazed at the milling crowd, seeing no one. The smaller object in the picture I recognized and the significance of the light corner was dawning on me. It was a different texture from the rock—it was fabric. Kay and I said it at the same time—the Ringers. We had both recognized the homespun material worn by the Ringers.

"And this," I pointed to the lower object, "is the toe of my shoe." Pushing my glasses higher on my nose, I gave the picture my extra close magnified scrutiny. My right foot, I though. I must have been out cold on my back.

"If Lew Weber took this picture he must have been unable to move you, Tish. Do you suppose he was hurt—broke his leg or something? He certainly wouldn't just sit taking pictures over your inert body unless he was some kind of monster."

"Let's think, Kay. I'm lying there. Lew can't move himself except to take pictures so he can't move me. The Ringers come, Lew takes this last picture, perhaps by mistake, they take Lew out of there and leave me. Why in Sam Hill would they do a thing like that?"

Kay said he must have taken the film out of his camera awfully quickly and planted it on me. But we wondered. Why just take Lew? Why take anyone? If the Ringers thought it was their private cave why not take us out, call the squad and ask us to quit trespassing?

"But we weren't trespassing, Kay. I'm sure that land belongs to me or to the Lawtons."

My head ached and I voted for a quick trip home. I wanted to tell Hilary what had happened. He had a way with untangling knots.

Rocking on my front porch, Hilary, looking like the Bard contemplating a tragedy, once again expressed his concern with irritable words.

"Peeked in, Tish. What a godawful mess. Do you always leave the house looking like that?"

My front door is always unlocked in the daytime. Kay rushed inside and instantly turned around.

"Holy Christmas, what a mess. They must have been looking for the film. The bastards. The dirty bastards."

It was a good thing I was wedged between Kay and the doorjamb. I felt my knees disengaging. Hilary led me to the wing chair and returned in a moment with a pony of brandy. I guess I drank it. I was too numb to feel it going down. But I did feel anger flooding my being, surging like foam from a pressure can.

Desk drawers were overturned and my carefully kept accounts and important documents were scattered all over the rug. Each of the six small drawers in the lowboy had been emptied. The most devastating sight was my cherished books swept from the shelves with brutal indifference.

Lulu's barking was bringing me close to the edge of hysteria. Hilary put her in my lap.

"Stay there," he commanded, "both of you."

I hugged Lulu, resting my forehead on her soft coat. This can't be happening in Lofton. My house invaded right here in my own town, right in the middle of Main Street. What fools we had been! Why had we let those dreadful Ringers bamboozle us?

19

Were Vermonters so naive? Did we really think that everyone wanted to enjoy Vermont, to love it, to cherish it? Hadn't we learned our lesson from the real estate developers—the creeping condos and all the others greedy for land for personal gain? Had we really been so stupid as to think some cult could be a good neighbor? I had to share the blame, since I was on the zoning board. My feelings of doubt about the Ringers had been overridden by others urging a broader tax base if we were to control Lofton's destiny. And, after all, it wasn't as though we were turning the town over to them. We'd all be here to monitor their activities. Too, Scarlett O'Hara, who sold the properties, had extolled the Ringers' virtues.

It never crossed my mind that the rats who had torn my house apart were other than the Marshal's disciples or that my analysis of the photograph taken in what Hilary called a root cellar could be wrong.

Kay reappeared. "The other rooms are untouched, thank goodness."

"Yeah," Hilary added, "this seems to be it." He began to pick up the books giving each one a reassuring pat as he placed it on the table. "Maybe I unwittingly scared them away."

"Or," Kay cocked her head, "They found what they were looking for right here in the living room."

That remark made my head pop up painfully. The surge I felt now was laughter. "Oh, no!" I hooted and heehawed while my friends watched me with nervous smiles. Kay's hand on my arm reminded me how close my tears, anger or laughter was to hysteria. Finally under control, I pointed to a striped canvas bag turned inside out. "I had a film in there. I was going to take it across the street to be developed this morning, but of course I didn't." I wiped my eyes enjoying the lovely exhaustion of laughter.

"What about the film, Tish?" Kay knelt beside me. "Tell us."

"You know the pamphlet I promised to illustrate for the Ladies Aid about Vermont cheese. Well, the whole roll is close-ups of Nancy Smithers milking her cow." We all laughed then.

Our amusement didn't last long. I was mortally tired. Hilary had a dentist appointment. Kay insisted I go into the study and rest. The study is a minuscule room Doug had used as an office. The couch there is my favorite napping spot. With the old afghan pulled up to my chin, I sighed with relief, though I knew it was just a matter of hours before I'd have to face demanding and frightening reality. Kay assured me that Ruth was at the gallery and loved running the place by herself, and that she would stay and clean up the living room. Dear kind friend, placing objects and books where she thought they belonged. I'd rearrange them later if I had the energy.

When Lulu curled up beside me on the couch, I saw she had adopted Lew's red kerchief. "A bloodhound," I yelled, "a bloodhound."

Kay looked in. She must have thought I'd gone mad. "Sure," she said, patting Lulu, "cute little bloodhound."

I tried to recall Lew's exact words. "He said he wished Lulu was a bloodhound so he could find the Ringers. That's what we need, Kay, a bloodhound to find Lew." I picked up the kerchief gingerly. "Put it in a plastic bag carefully, though it probably smells more like Lulu than Lew by now."

Faint feelings of hope helped me drift off to sleep.

3

Lulu was no longer beside me when I wakened. I could hear Kay talking in the living room.

"I had a lump in my throat looking at her today, Terry. She looked so old."

"But she's a tough old party. How old is she?"

When Kay replied I knew they were talking about me. Old? God knows I felt old today with cracked ribs and an aching head uneasily perched on a stiff neck. But old? What nonsense! Look at Harry What's-his-name shaking hands with wellwishers on his hundredth. Sixty-five wasn't old any more.

Kay was talking. "You know, from the time Tish walked in opening day at the gallery she's been an inspiration. No kidding." I imagined Terry must have made a face or muttered an uncomplimentary remark. "Really, her help, her energy and her incredible ingenuity." I liked this part of the conversation better. "I hate to see her so beat up, so upset."

Then I could partly hear, but not follow, a discussion about bloodhounds and the police. Police first, I thought, as I brushed my hair. I'd call Charles Reed, our new young state trooper, and talk to him about the vandals. Then I'd call Lew Weber's paper. I hoped with all my heart they'd say hold the line, he's right here, but my doubts were profound.

Terry Fink had gone back to the Inn when I came

into the living room. It looked tidier than when we had left for Rutland this morning. Kay was on the porch perched on the railing, her head against the post. She's the one I should be painting, not all those monied clients she produced. Her ivory skin and pink cheeks and honey hair wound in a straggly knot at the nape of her neck was evocative of the work of nineteenth century English painters. Her figure was a little more lush than current fashion allowed, certainly the only old-fashioned thing about her. I wondered if thinking of Terry was responsible for her dreamy expression. In spite of the fact that Terry was a tennis whiz, a world class skier and a much sought-after bachelor, to me he lacked some basic virility and my dirty old mind wondered if his relationship with Martin Brown was more than a business one, as co-owners of the Lofton Inn.

I thumbed through the yellow pages and found a number for Lew's paper—or was it his paper? They had never heard of Lew Weber. I called other papers and magazines with the same negative responses.

"Tish," Kay said, "could Lew Weber be a real stinker? Could he have left you lying unconscious in that place, in that dungeon?"

"Do you know anyone that horrible?" I said. "I don't."

I dialed again and Officer Reed responded on his car telephone and said he was nearby and would be with me in ten minutes.

Kay went over to the store and I put the kettle on for tea. In spite of my lack of interest in cooking, I loved my kitchen. The walls were pale pansy yellow with curtains to match. The counter tops were white and the cabinets and woodwork Vermont maple. Doug had loved copper pots and pans and while I hardly ever used them, they looked great hanging from an iron oval dropped from the ceiling. My real love I saved for the brick floor. I had laboriously massaged each brick with axle grease, the recipe of a nutty old purist Doug had fallen for at some antique show. The other side of the kitchen opened into my studio. Thank goodness the Ringers hadn't started their search there.

The kettle's whistle and a knock on the door got me moving.

"Come in, Charlie, be there in a minute."

I had known our police officer ever since we came to Lofton. As a youngster he had helped his father mow our back field every summer and he had often been my cheerful assistant in many outdoor chores. My confidence in him as a human being was boundless, but to think of him as a mature officer of the law was difficult for me to manage. His youthful appearance did nothing to assuage my doubts. If Charlie Reed were a mugger, it would be difficult to describe him to the police. He was so medium. His light brown hair was precisely trimmed with sideburns a touch too long for my taste. His gray eyes, height and shape were average. His smile managed to look serious. I knew his good manners were innate.

No tea, he said the caffeine was bad for him but he accepted a glass of ginger ale. He held it up. "Diet?"

I assured him that it was a low calorie potion, and we settled down as I tried to recreate the last twenty-four hours as accurately as I could. He was a good listener—I'll say that for him. Finally, I handed him the snapshot of my foot and the Ringers' cloth with no comment.

"The toe of a shoe," he said, "is that yours?" I

24

nodded. "And the corner here was light struck, I guess."

Then I told him Kay's and my explanation. He shrugged.

"Might have put his thumb on the lens by mistake. Might not be cloth."

When I handed him the rest of the photographs he rose and took them to the window and with great care examined each one. His rising excitement was palpable.

"Do realize what these are, Mrs. McWhinny, these markings on the rocks?" I shook my head (I remembered to do it very slowly). "These marks were made by the Celts or the Druids about 300 A.D."

Nobody looks her best with her mouth agape, so I closed it.

"Do you realize what you've done? Do you know what this means?" He waved the pictures over his head like a victor's check. "Do you know what this is?"

"What are you talking about?"

"I'll tell you what you did, Mrs. McWhinny. You fell into a Druid temple."

"You're pulling my leg, Charlie."

His face was flushed and he seemed to be rising up and down on his toes as though preparing for flight. "Wait till they see these pictures!!"

"The Druids?" I asked politely.

"No, no, our archaeology club in Claremont." He consulted his Rolex Oyster. "Darn, I have to talk to some Boy Scouts in Bondville in half an hour so we can't go to the temple now. I'll be off duty tomorrow, Mrs. McWhinny, and I'll be here at noon, okay?"

My echoing okay floated after him as he flew out the door. Not a word about the vandals, the film. No mention of Lew Weber. Charlie had been transported. A temple! I pushed aside my tea cup and decided to switch to scotch.

Hilary barged in the door holding a covered casserole that smelled delicious. Once mistaken for Bing Crosby at some drunken college reunion, he was given to rendering appropriate songs.

"Supper time," he sang, "time to set the table."

My frog-like alto supplied the next line. "Supper time, but somehow I'm not able."

"What's the matter, Tish? You look sort of cross-eyed. Don't blame you. That was one hell of a shock seeing this room torn apart. Hey, it looks great now."

His monologue lasted until Kay appeared. She put down a bag of groceries and sniffed the casserole. "Enough for me, I hope."

Hilary took her arm and nodded in my direction and said softly, "She doesn't look so good." The notion that anyone who didn't feel well was automatically deaf irritated me.

"Listen, you two. About the root cellar—I was right. There is no root cellar. You know what I fell into?" I waited until I had their undivided attention. "I fell into a Druid temple!"

They quickly turned their heads and whispered for a second. I put out my hand and stopped Hilary as he reached for the telephone.

"Just thought we might invite Doc over for a drink," he said.

After I had convinced them I was in possession of my wits and senses, I described Charlie's reaction to the pictures and told them what he had said.

Kay was enthralled. Hilary kept hitting his forehead with the heel of his hand.

"Why didn't I see it? Of course, of course. I've

even seen those rock structures in Woodstock. Charlie may be right, Tish. Plenty of scholars and archeologists are trying to prove that Celts and Druids came to New England."

Kay's wheels were whirling. "We'll have an exhibition of Celtic rocks. I can see it now. Maybe I'll start a museum. Maybe right there at the temple. I know, I'll call it the Temple. I can see it now—huge phallic rocks on either side of the front door, like Pompeii."

Kay rambled on and Hilary tried to remember what he'd seen in Woodstock while I barely tasted his fine food. I was exhausted. When my kind friends took a minute to look at me, they left full of admonitions and advice for my safety and well being.

With the house locked and my watch dog asleep in my lap, I pined for a cigarette. A reformed smoker, I wondered why I was bucking for immortality. Did I really want a horseshoe like what's-his-name? There were certain times when a cigarette was indispensable to the cognitive process and this was one of those times.

Why did I worry about Lew Weber? Probably he was having a beer with chums in a bar in Springfield, or was fast asleep in a motel in Hardwick or—what really bothered me—was lying hurt somewhere, hurt and possibly a captive of the Ringers. But why? Just because the Ringers weren't appealing didn't mean they were evil. Were they the ones responsible for that phone call? Charlie and Hilary didn't seem concerned about Lew. Even Kay seemed to have forgotten him in the flurry of excitement about Celts and Druids and pagan temples.

Lulu grunted as I moved suddenly. What a horrid thought. I was the only person to have seen Lew Weber. Neither the Macys at the store nor anyone at the post office had seen him. No one saw his car. Except for my toe, the film could have been shot by anyone. Lots of people wore L.L. Bean moccasins. Maybe it wasn't even my foot. And Lew's kerchief was one of a million in Vermont, sold at every country store and beloved by campers.

Then I started thinking about Alan Smith, better known as The Marshal. His vanity singled him out from his followers. He fancied ornamentation. His costume, also home spun, was drawn in around his middle by a heavy chain belt. The matching gold chain around his neck served as a key ring. A gold whistle shared its chain with an object which appeared to be a small gold and ivory dagger. Those who had a closer look thought it was a phallus. He constantly fondled whatever it was, and he often appeared with the whistle in his mouth. Perhaps, I thought with a flash of sympathy, he's trying to quit smoking.

His disciples wore knee-length beige homespun shirts over khaki pants which, though they may have been clean, managed to look wrinkled and grubby. Nothing distinguished them from the rest of the population except their drab costumes and unsmiling faces.

Did the Marshal forbid smiling? Was punishment prescribed for a laugh?

We had all read the uninspiring, uninformative flyer produced by the Ringers for local distribution. It extolled the planting and harvesting of one's own food, and seemed to be cribbed from a seed catalogue.

Why should their devotion to the fruits of the earth produce such dour and dreary behavior? Why should pulling carrots make you so grim?

According to Marge, the rare times a Ringer came into the store it wasn't to buy wine or cigarettes, but candy and soft drinks.

Unless someone was able to develop a rapport between the townspeople and the Ringers, perhaps we'd never know what made them tick. A few gregarious and friendly Loftonites had tried, but with no success.

The church program committee had already made overtures and reported a curt brush-off. A peppy villager, Mary Hanson, wasn't accustomed to rejection, which is just what she got when she invited Smith to a cocktail party. Lucy White vowed to sell them chances for the benefit of the fire department. Greatly to her surprise, Smith sent a disciple down with a twenty dollar bill and bought the whole book of chances. The joker in that performance was that the winner of the raffle could claim a portrait painted by me! Lucy made me promise that if The Marshal won, I'd let her come along as my assistant, though the only time I required such was as a reader for restless children. But that was last month and the drawing wasn't until Labor Day.

Jean Small, the district nurse, held an extremely biased view of the Ringers. A disciple of the god (or goddess) of cleanliness herself, she shuddered when she thought of their dirty toenails. Though she had never entered the portals of Amber Trees (which is what we all still called the place) she based her observations on roadside encounters.

Pete, who ran the village garage, had rubbed his dry, callused hands together, which was as close as he ever came to a gesture of greed, at the thought of servicing the Ringers' megabuck cars. But he was disappointed. Not really, he confided to me. "I have

29

plenty to do just taking care of my friends, and besides, all their cars are foreign." He concluded there must be mechanics among the disciples.

The Swallows, who kept horses, were outspoken about the Ringers. Birdie Swallow, the Wagnerian madam of the stable, said she'd damn near killed her beloved Arabian as well as herself running into a fence that crossed a trail on what she had always regarded as public land.

Lizzie Bell said before she went to Europe that if the Ring of Righters were anything like the organization of yogis she knew in New York, they would be kind, friendly and industrious. I shared her feelings about yogis. After Doug died, I'd thrown myself into a winter of late afternoon yoga classes. It took care of that lonely time of day we had always shared. I still practiced yoga, but it wasn't the same without the mindless luxury of an instructor telling you what to do. The young woman Lew and I had seen standing on her head had momentarily made me feel better about the Ringers.

It was impossible not to compare them to other cults. People shuddered when they discussed horrors like Jonestown. Many drew a parallel to the guru Ragneesh, the Rolls Royce devotee who had established a town in Oregon, and had been banished by the immigration authorities. His cult's practices were based on Eastern philosophies and popular appeal and attracted a well-heeled and well-educated group. They weren't especially secretive and seemed full of good cheer. We laughed at his decree that made love-making with rubber gloves imperative. Along with old-time venereal diseases, I suppose they were trying to avoid herpes and probably AIDS. Pete's wife Lucy, as the only Loftonite to breach the Ringers' portal when she sold them the Fire Department chances, was asked if this were true. She squealed with delight and assured us that in spite of having stood on their front porch for five minutes, she had been propositioned by none of the Ringers.

If, for whatever reason, Lew Weber was being held by the Ringers, how would they treat him? Would he be smoking a joint with the Marshal, or locked in a cellar closet?

A reluctant pill popper, I wrestled the top off the plastic cylinder and washed down another magic capsule.

4

My teapot and mug were upside down on the drain board along with Lulu's dish, which featured a picture of a kitten—an embarrassing reminder that I should avoid impulse buying when I don't have my glasses on.

Charlie was prompt. This morning he was not Charlie Reed the State Trooper, but Charles Reed the archaeologist. He looked quite dashing in high-laced boots over army fatigues and a safari jacket. He wore both a camera and a knapsack. A picnic lunch, I wondered?

"Whew! What a morning! My mother-in-law got a speeding ticket in Springfield and is having hysterics. My little boy's kitten is up in a birch tree and he's sitting under it waiting for the fire truck to come and rescue it. Then my car wouldn't start. Amazing I'm here."

I was amazed, not that Charlie had arrived in spite of his trying morning, but that he was old enough to be a husband and the father of a child old enough to own a kitten.

"How old are you, Charlie?"

"Twenty-six. Old enough to drink coffee. I could use a cup of the real thing."

I filled the kettle and slid some English muffins in

the toaster and put marmalade and mugs on the table.

Charlie was leafing through a slim book he'd removed from his pocket. "Look at this." He flattened the book on the table and pointed. Hieroglyphics weren't my field.

"Early Esperanto?"

"This is Ogam script, the alphabet of the ancient Celtic language. Ogam inscriptions are what we are finding now all over New England. Where are the pictures of your temple?"

My temple! An ancient cave, maybe, but a temple? I smiled at Charlie's happy, eager face and handed him the snapshots which he studied.

With coffee and muffins on the table I invited Charlie to tell me more. Archaeology had never been of any particular interest to me. I assumed that American digs produced only Indian arrowheads and flint stones. In Vermont, the Indian artifacts which had been found were attributed to the Abenakis, Algonquins and Iroquois. Charlie said that the new wave of archeologists believe that the Celts were here about 300 B.C. Ogam inscriptions in caves and incised Ogam words on standing rocks were the proof of this assumption. "There are plenty of skeptics. Most archeologists say the chambers are root cellars and the stone markings are the result of erosion, or scars made by hauling tools and other natural abrasions."

"And you believe these caves—root cellars—are Celtic temples?"

"A cave is a natural rock formation. These chambers, no matter what they were used for, are manmade. Of course I want to believe the Celts were here. Even the sternest critics who claim that there

33

is no evidence of pre-Colombian settlers add that of course something could turn up in the future. Plenty of them admit they don't know what some inscriptions mean. So I vote for Ogam. We have a little club. We track down clues. They'll go crazy then they see your temple. Let's go."

To mince along at my invalid pace obviously was painful for Charlie, but I was grateful for the support of his arm. Just as we cleared the rise before descending to the cave site, we both stopped suddenly, but only for a split second. I gasped at the brutal scene below. Charlie tore off his camera and slipped out of his knapsack in one atavistic twist and leapt off the hill. He hit the rough turf below running. He threw himself in the middle of an already crowded battlefield consisting of two Ringers and a man in shorts.

A Ringer's flowing homespun swirled around in the wild free-for-all and hid much of the action. I recognized Terry Fink's blond hair. His bare legs were kicking like a trip hammer and his fists were pounding ineffectually. The obscenities he offered seemed warranted in this shamefully unequal struggle.

Charlie's arrival changed the balance of power dramatically. He clutched one Ringer's beard. I almost laughed when it came off in his hand. He then punched him in the stomach. The man sank to his knees gagging. Charlie whirled around and, in a deft display of karate, kicked the other Ringer under the chin. He fell to the ground like a plank.

Terry, on his hands and knees, shook his head like a dog. Charlie knelt beside him. "Okay, Terry?"

Terry nodded. He was still muttering threatening epithets.

"What happened?" Charlie asked. "What's this all about?" He helped Terry to his feet and introduced himself to each Ringer. When he repeated his name, Office Reed of the Vermont State Police, they didn't respond.

Terry explained that he had heard about the cave (from Kay, of course) and had come to see it a little while ago. No sooner had he found the place than the Ringers appeared and ordered him to leave. When Terry refused, they attacked him.

It seemed to me that there must have been more provocation than Terry described to produce such violence. I squinted at Terry for a new look. Compared to the rumpled Ringers, he looked like a smooth Greek god or a slim gladiator. For the first time I could see why Kay found him intriguing. In seconds he changed from an angry warrior back to the urbane and clever innkeeper I knew.

"They said they owned the land," Terry said, "but they don't. You do, don't you, Tish?"

I looked around me. "I think so."

He wiped a bloody hand on his tee shirt and managed a smile.

"Glad you brought black belt Charlie along, Tish. It felt sort of like curtains to me. Those thugs play tough and dirty."

Sprawled on the ground, they looked like a couple of Bowery bums. In spite of my distaste for the miserable creatures, I realized they needed attention.

"Charlie, shall I go call the rescue squad?"

Before he could reply, four more Ringers appeared. One, a woman, dropped to her knees between the men. She sent me a look of pure venom. "How could you!"

"Me?" I asked in astonishment.

She turned her head to include Charlie and Terry. "You pigs." I guess they didn't worship pigs.

Always one for putting things in perspective, I offered, "Your friends attacked Mr. Fink. He was alone. Two against one," I added piously.

An older Ringer spoke with a voice of authority. "Please leave us. You are trespassing on private property."

"We'll leave," Terry said, "but get this straight, all of you. This is not your property."

Even though I felt a strong urge to add my two bits about land ownership, I kept quiet.

Charlie added, "Tell your leader to expect me in a few minutes, and you four be there too."

Afraid of another fracas, I fluttered around and pulled Charlie's arm. He in turn prodded Terry's back. Charlie needed an extra tug. I could imagine his bitter disappointment at having to postpone his examination of the Druid temple. So near and yet so . . . Oh well, we could get someone to open the town hall and check the boundaries and be back in no time.

We were outnumbered by the grumbling Ringers and I was relieved when Charlie retrieved his belongings and we crossed over the hill and headed back to town.

There was plenty of action in Lofton on Saturday. Dogs frolicked with their pintsized owners. People pushed in and out of the store's screen door. This was French bread day and a long loaf stuck out of almost every grocery bag. The post office was busy and beside the store a tourist was kicking the world's worst ice bag machine.

Our postmaster, Herb, who usually knew where everybody was, was spending the day with his niece in Brattleboro. Lucy White, our town clerk, didn't answer her phone. Scarlett O'Hara had a key to the town hall but Saturday was usually a busy day for her. She was the enthusiastic realtor who had arranged the sale of Amber Trees and the other properties to the Ringers, and she was probably striking a big deal right now on some pasture land gone to seed.

There was no way to see the town map right now, and the file of deeds was locked up in the new concrete vault. Terry looked in all four windows to see if the wall map was visible, but with no success.

I found myself warming to this young man. Young? Perhaps he was 35, 40? He had handled himself well and for someone who was pounced upon by two much larger men he had shown a lot of gumption. I urged him to go back to the inn .

"You need a shower, Terry, and a box of bandaids. The way you look, you'd probably scare off your luncheon crowd." Impulsively I added, "Please come see me soon."

There was no decent time when you could call on an innkeeper or ask an innkeeper to call. They were busy before, during and after meals, which left a scant hour in the middle of the morning or afternoon, when most other industrious people don't like to be bothered.

Terry switched the invitation. "You come for dinner at the inn tonight, Tish. Kay's coming."

I wondered how Kay would like that arrangement. Maybe I should invite Hilary, too. An invitation from Marty or Terry to dine at the inn didn't mean they were paying the tab. It usually meant a free liqueur, often a mysterious fruity draft that guaranteed a four a.m. hangover. So I had no qualms about asking Hilary. I promised myself to call him later.

"Charlie, when you see The Marshal give him hell

for me. I think it's disgraceful to let his thugs beat up anyone, on their property or mine."

Charlie said, "The Ringers clearly think it belongs to them."

I wasn't going to argue that point until I saw my deed.

"Please ask about Lew Weber, Charlie. We must find him." Just thinking about him made my head hurt.

"But we don't know that he's missing, Mrs. McWhinny. We just have your word for it." I didn't like that "just". "There's been no missing persons alert and we have no right to just barge in there and search. And you told me that Lofton was his first stop of possibly many." Charlie said he'd return to see the temple tomorrow, Sunday. He'd telephone when he found out about his assignments and duties.

Dispirited and tired I trudged over to the store to talk to Marge and Kevin. An endearing pair. Marge was merry, talkative and plump. How all those M & M's she used as a daily fix stayed on her hips I don't know. She ran, she scampered and she skipped, and often made change before you handed her your money. Kevin was Jack Spratt, tall and narrow. His Adam's apple was his most prominent feature and his most usual utterance was "betcha". I've never figured our how such a skimpy, quiet person could exude such warmth.

Miraculously the store was empty, except for Marge and Kevin. Slumped in the director's chair by the stove, I moaned. "I used to think I was a reasonable, tolerant woman, fair and unbiased, but I'm not—I'm full of hate. I hate the bastards. I just hate them."

Kevin's head cocked in a quizzical pose. "Now let

me guess. Don't tell me. You hate those benign disciples of the Ring of Right."

They gave me their total attention for the review of my experiences. I told them everything—about Lew, the cave, the film, the vandals and this morning's battle.

Marge settled on the Druid temple as the most interesting part of my saga. She suggested, "When you go up to the temple or cave tomorrow why don't you take a lot of people with you. The Ringers wouldn't dare start anything and at least you'd get to see the place." Marge deserved her reputation for good advice.

A kiss was planted firmly on my cheek. I caught my glasses just in time. I greeted Walter Upson with equal warmth. Walter was the manager of the Lofton Corporation. A youngish bachelor, he lived in a brown shingle house near the ski area that looked too tiny to contain this ebullient shaggy bear of a man.

"Hi, gorgeous, hear you've been messing around with a young man who hit you over the head. Where is he?" Walter had a great growl. "I'll kill him."

"If you can find him, dear heart, I'm about ready to suggest you do just that." Then of course I had to tell Walter all about my last 48 hours. Except for a few growls he didn't interrupt but thank goodness he expressed some concern about Lew Weber.

News reporting had been among Walter's many previous pursuits and he offered to call some Vermont papers and periodicals that I probably had missed. I was gratified to know that he didn't think anyone would be rotten enough to leave me lying in a cave.

"Will I see you at the inn tonight?"

Loftonites loved to eat at the inn on Saturday

night. The boys—Marty and Terry had been called that from the day they arrived—offered a twelve dollar special on Maine lobster that was irresistible.

Walter lent me his arm for the walk home. A kind and perceptive fellow, as The Lofton Corporation's new manager he had made an instant hit with old and young alike and seemed to have a genuine concern for our interests. With the onslaught of heedless developers and their greedy ancillary troops, his attitude was most welcome.

You would think I was old enough to resist the allure of an attractive young male, but I guess you're never too old. I might as well have crushed my glasses underfoot for all the good they did when I looked at Walter. Did Kay know him? I rather enjoyed matchmaking. You old fool, I thought. Don't forget that, in spite of his considerable charms, good taste and winning ways, we are on different teams.

I knew that Walter's job was to expand the corporation's holdings, enlarge the parking areas, add a few more ski lifts and build another lodge and restaurant. Though there wasn't much land left to exploit in Lofton, a few choice small chunks remained, one of which belonged to Hilary. The Lofton Corporation was desperately trying to buy his acreage. The huge sum of money they offered Hilary just made him shrug. If the corporation owned it, he reasoned, it would be clear-cut for skiers and become another perpendicular field. He said he wanted to keep the property as an R & R area for raccoons, skunks and porcupines. His whimsy failed to infect his tight-lipped suitors.

The Ottauquechee Land Trust Society and the Nature Conservancy were choices we discussed as protectors of the land.

"Has Hilary decided what to do with his land on the mountain?" Walter asked me.

Either my skull was getting transparent or the wrinkles on my brow sent messages in Ogam, but everyone seemed to be able to read my mind.

"We haven't discussed it lately." (Probably not for two whole days.) As well as transparent, I was getting to be a full time liar.

5

The scar that went from the center of my right thumb to my wrist attested to the fact that I had once lost a battle with a Maine lobster. There was no danger tonight—the battle tonight had been won before I got there, there were no claws to crack. The way they prepared lobster, as well as the price at the inn, accounted for the crowded dining room and the people waiting in the bar.

Marty Brown, Terry's partner, had given Hilary the recipe for Lofty lobster: plunge a live lobster into boiling water for ten minutes. Remove and twist off claws and joints and add the meat to a stuffing made of crushed pilot crackers, parsley, lemon juice, a shake of Worcestershire and ketchup and lots of melted butter. Stuff the lobster and cover with foil. Bake in a pan with a little water in the bottom. Bake at 350° for 20 minutes. Uncover and bake ten more minutes at 400°. You may want even more melted butter for dunking.

Kay was retrieving a chunk of claw meat from her butter bowl when she caught me smiling and waving at Walter Upson. "Who's the grizzly?" She mopped her buttery chin.

The tone of her question irritated me. In my opinion Walter was ten or twenty times more attractive than Terry. What if he did have a lousy barber—I took another look at him—or no barber? And of course there was always the question of a beard hiding a weak chin. Before I could explain Walter's charm to Kay, Terry, with hands folded behind his back, bent over and said quietly, "Tish, that guy over in the corner looks like one of the guys who jumped me. What do you think?"

I saw who he meant. In the far corner a man with dark hair and a square face was unfolding his napkin. I shook my head. While one of Terry's assailants wore a fake beard, he had a pointed head and the other one, though dark, had an oval face, not square. The thought that either of them would be dining at the inn startled me. Did they leave their togas at home, scrub their toes and sally forth in mufti in the evening? Improbable was our collective decision.

We agreed to have a liqueur with Terry after dinner in the bar. "But let's not hurry," Kay inhaled her espresso. "The inn makes more money from drinks than food. I hope Terry can sit down with us, but Martin's away and he's in charge of everything."

Martin, Terry's extremely silent partner, was in charge of the kitchen, dining room and marketing. Kay explained he had taken a few weeks off to work at the Culinary Institute down on the Hudson. A slight, shy fellow, he accepted compliments about the inn's fare with a rueful smile as though your dinner had been a happy accident that might not occur again.

Walter almost singed his beard on the candle when he bent over to invite us for a drink. "Let me buy you a brandy before Terry gives us a Lofton special eau de vie."

He escorted us to a table in the bar. Standing behind the bar, Terry exhibited the green-eyed look of jealousy. I'd observed the instant pain of jealousy often telegraphed by an almost imperceptible tightening of muscles around the eyes. Also noticeable on Terry's face was a twitch at the hinge of his jaw bone. Jealous of Kay? I doubted that. More likely the source of his irritation was that Walter's massive intrusion had robbed Terry of his role of host. Maybe it wasn't jealousy but resentment. But he recovered his urbane and cultivated manner and erased my fleeting impression. He came over and graciously offered all of us our choice of a liqueur.

"Hear you mopped up the turf with some Ringers yesterday." Walter raised his brandy glass to Terry. "Good show."

"Karate Charlie made quite a difference. Tish, let's go up and really examine that place tomorrow. They wouldn't dare bother us again, no matter who owns the land."

"I've been in a lot of caves, but not in Vermont," Walter said. "Prehistoric caves."

"You fancy bats?" Kay asked.

"They don't even let mosquitoes in some I've seen. Like Lascaux."

"You've seen it?" she asked. Walter nodded. Terry pulled out a chair and waved to Jenny, a summer helper, to take over the bar. "Is it more exciting than Altamira?"

"Smaller and, yeah, really exciting."

"That's right," I added. "You just came back from France. Tell us."

"Now?" Walter looked around the table. We all nodded.

"The grotto itself is just beyond a great little town. We ate lunch at this inn." Walter rolled his eyes. "We had . . ."

44

"Oh, come on." I patted his arm. "Describe lunch later."

"We rang a bell fastened to a high no-nonsense fence which didn't seem to be protecting anything except possibly a little gatehouse. We could smell a Gauloise before we saw this guy. Some casting director had chosen well. He must have been over fifty, dark haired, his coat collar turned up." Walter turned his collar up. "You'd have swooned, Tish."

"Tell us about the cave, for heavens sake. I've done my swooning for this season."

"We stopped first in the gatehouse. Our French was lousy so we had to concentrate on the instructions. No cameras, no knapsacks or bags and no talking in the cave. Said he'd answer questions afterwards. We followed him across a clearing and into an enclosure where a metal door was opened. We had to walk through the doorway and then through a trough of disinfectant. The cave was discovered forty years ago by two brothers running around in the woods. When their dog vanished, the boys, led on by her barking, fell into the cave with her, tumbling back thirty thousand years in time. They ran to school and returned with their teacher who called a famous historian who lived nearby. He examined the cave with a borrowed torch and proclaimed it the Sistine Chapel of prehistoric art. It was sealed, but the guy who lent him the torch was a resistance leader and he stored munitions in the cave. This was in the middle of the Second World War so you can imagine it didn't rate very high in order of importance in national news. Soon this most important archeological find since God knows when got treated like any old tourist attraction. Anyone could come in for a look. Took about ten years for the government to realize that this priceless treasure was deteriorating.

"The breath of sightseers had begun to erode the transparent mineral deposit that preserved the paintings all those years. Since then only a few people a day are admitted and that has to be planned well in advance.

"After the foot bath, we followed Pierre's flashlight down a handful of steps. At the bottom we stood for a minute in the dark. Then he pulled on a bare light bulb hanging from the roof and looked at us. "Voila." He gave us a couple of minutes to catch our breath.

"The paintings. What can I tell you? It's a mind blower. The colors on those creamy walls—the black looks as fresh as velvet and the earth colors—you could describe it better that I can, Tish."

"How did they make the paint?" Terry asked.

"Same way purists still do," I said. "Grind minerals and oxides, add oil or fat, I guess. I'm lazy. I squeeze it out of horrid plastic tubes."

"The animals! There's a bull 12 feet long and the cave there is only 12 feet wide—what an impact! But it's the feeling you get of being transported through history," Walter said. "And those guys could really draw."

"Guys?" Kay asked. "How do you know?"

He touched an imaginary visor. "Those people could draw."

"The women were probably the hunters, too," Kay added, "but do go on."

"Back in the gate house we collected our belongings. I shook hands with our guide and in my high school French asked a question. I had guessed the answer. I asked, 'Were you one of the brothers who found the cave?' 'Oui,' he smiled. 'Je m'appel Jacques Marsal.'

We were quiet for a moment. My spine tingled. I was ready to pack a bag and book a flight to France.

Hilary put his hand on mine and gave it a squeeze. "Like you, Tish. You fell into Lofton's greatest archeological site."

"Lofton's only archeological site," Kay said, "but from the snapshots I've seen it's not very hot competition for Lascaux."

"How do we know it's the only cave," Terry beamed. "Maybe there are others. My God, what a treasure hunt we'll have."

"Chamber, Terry." I parroted Charlie. "A cave is a natural formation."

"What a tourist attraction," Walter added, ever the promoter. "I can see it now—a convention of archeologists in the middle of mud season. We may have to give you a cut, Tish, or maybe you want to rig up your own turnstile and collect the shekels yourself."

Had I discovered a monster that would devour Lofton and regurgitate it in a form we'd all hate?

"Cool it." I held up both palms. "Wait until tomorrow. Then we'll call Heman Chase to check out the boundaries." Heman was everyone's favorite surveyor.

While Lofton's archeological possibilities were discussed in a merry haze of euphoria, I thought about Lew Weber. He knew about Lofty's chamber, temple, root cellar, whatever it was. Where was he? I couldn't get him out of my mind. To bring up his disappearance now I knew would evoke the usual recommendation not to worry—to forget him.

"You'll hear something about the boy soon."

Had I said anything? Hilary was reading my mind again.

I hugged my ribs gently and told my eager friends that I wasn't up to arranging an assault of the town hall tomorrow and I didn't have the pep to confront the Ringers about property lines. Hilary insisted on taking me home and suggested we all meet after church tomorrow—12 noon on the church steps.

Why the rest of the congregation looked so happy in church I don't really know. Did each person have a special reason for attending our simple Sunday services? Was it in appreciation of the lovely building? Loyalty to our sweet aged minister? Or a deep commitment to Christian principles? For me it was a refreshing interlude from work, a time to feel serene and let my eyes feast on the satisfying proportions of the altar and to admire the wild flowers arranged by knowing hands. I enjoyed seeing the children and watching Herb's knotty old hands on the organ keyboard, but I saw none of that today. Dread for the possible scene with the Ringers had me in its thrall. It wasn't fair just because I was in a church to call what I wished a prayer, but I closed my eyes and pleaded, please let that damn Druid temple turn out to be a plain old root cellar. The miserable vision of a parking lot full of tourists all traipsing across my land made me feel sick.

A sense of where I was returned when the minister, Mr. McQuade, asked if there were any community announcements to be made. Carlos Denver, in charge of maintenance, informed us of a problem with the clapboards on the north side of the building.

I gasped when the idea hit me. Of course—the congregation could be my body guards. I stood up.

"Perhaps you've heard . . ." Then I told them about falling in the rocky hole. I didn't mention Lew but I said that the Ring of Right thought it belonged to them. However, I thought now was the time for Loftonites to examine the site. Yes, right after church.

Poor Mr. McQuade. The congregation could hardly sit through the sermon. I hope the words he left out weren't indispensable for our spiritual well-being. Constantly consulting his watch, he managed to finish the service way ahead of schedule.

Onward Christian Soldiers sounded like an appropriate marching song for the excited congregation. I expected someone to appear with a flag at any moment. Charlie was already standing on the church steps, his uniform adding the right touch. Hilary and I followed at my pace.

"O'Hara looks as though she'd just lost her best friend," Hilary observed. Our prominent local realtor certainly didn't move on tippy toes, her usual gait, or swing her mop of red hair to catch the light, nor did she usually walk alone. I only fleetingly wondered at her uncharacteristic behavior.

When the explosion occurred, the front of our group was about one hundred feet short of the rock chamber. Even ten feet closer, most agreed, would have resulted in tragic injuries. Even so, the leaders and the next dozen people behind them were on their knees. Mr. McQuade was clutching a tree trunk. Scarlet O'Hara had sunk to the ground. I watched as Terry revived her. Back on her feet, she clung to his arm.

Charlie and Walter were the first to move forward. Amazingly enough, Hilary and I were right behind them. About twenty Ringers were standing beyond the mounds of earth and rock tossed up by the explosion. They appeared to be waiting for the class photographer. Alan Smith stepped forward and raised his hands. No, it must be choir practice.

I felt giddy. Hilary hooked his arm in mine and spoke to the Ringers.

"What in hell do you think you're doing?"

Charlie walked toward the Ringers with his hand on his holster. The whole congregation moved in to fill the space behind him. Their vocal indignation made a menacing rumble. Alan Smith, Marshal, raised his hands again and tried a smile.

"Just a little blasting, folks. We're starting the foundation for a storage building."

My voice rose above the rest. "On my property?"

Then everyone started to talk at once. I did the sensible thing—I fainted. I don't think of myself as the fluttering fainting type, but the explosion was the last straw. My equilibrium was shattered.

Hilary hoisted me up and turned me over to the Calders, who were anxious to leave. They escorted me to my house.

The Calders got me a glass of sherry and practically pushed me into my wing chair. When they left, I didn't even try to move. Lulu's snores played an oblogato to my thoughts.

The Ringers had more in mind than building when they blasted the chamber. How much simpler it would have been to remove the stones by hand, or use what existed and build above the ancient foundation. They had probably destroyed whatever value the stones had to an archaeologist. Surely rocks nearest to the charge must have been shattered, or at least split.

Hilary had told me that the big chamber in South Woodstock and nearby rocks with provocative shapes and markings were unguarded and he said graffiti were on the increase and a large house had just been built within 200 yards of the rock site. "And for all we know," Hilary said, "a contractor might right now be planning a rustic swimming pool to be made out of marked stones. Why can't some bright character come up with some positive proof that the Celts or Druids built these chambers and wrote on those rocks?"

Charlie had added that archeology rarely had absolute certainties. What is thought of as the truth of an archeological site or area is what is considered most probable.

Since my fall into the darned Druid temple I had felt miserable, ineffectual and always on the verge of tears. And fainting—what a mess. My aching body commanded me to retreat. My instinctive withdrawal was later reinforced by my doctor's advice.

"Give up," he said. "Go to bed, cut off the phone, give in, let your ribs mend, try to be idle for once in your life."

Hibernation was what it looked like but rumination was more accurate. The old bones I put to bed, but the old bean kept churning.

Kay said she'd postpone my portrait job. She wanted to dash right over the mountain and hold my hand. Or Terry's, I thought sourly. I guess every part of me needed to recuperate, including my disposition.

Dear, understanding Hilary put the paper and my mail and a few groceries on the porch every morning of my retreat. When he left, I'd reach out and retrieve them like some furtive recluse.

For four days my state was one of total inertia. Sleep, baths, soup, more sleep. Lulu was in heaven. On the fifth day I felt a tiny infusion of vitality coursing through my veins. The sixth day I stretched to my full height (five feet six inches). Gently I palpated my ribs. I wasn't about to hog anyone's trampoline, but the pain was manageable.

Hilary made a grand occasion of my debut. With a chicken in the oven we settled down with our drinks and a half pound of smoked salmon surrounded by capers, cut lemon and fingers of pumpernickel.

Hilary was full of stored-up information.

Charlie had told Hilary that Smith actually apologized for the battle Saturday, said that his lieutenant in charge of the grounds had been overly zealous in his duties. Many of his flock, he explained, came from the city and felt strongly about defending their turf.

After the explosion, Charlie took charge of the dialogue. No matter who owned the property, he warned the Ringers, the town zoning laws did not allow any building within 75 feet of a boundary line. No one was permitted to use explosives without a permit. "He just slapped their hands," Hilary said.

When the Ringers retreated, Charlie had fallen to his knees beside a slab of rock tossed out by the dynamite. The markings on it were clear to Charlie—clearly Ogam script. Terry examined a long stone etched with other symbols. At least half the congregation stayed to look at the rocks. Mr. McQuade must have been happy to see so many of his flock on their knees. There were no skeptics. Everyone was enthralled with the discoveries.

The next day Charlie called the governor's office

and secured a promise to send an archaeologist down to examine the site.

"The whole town is in the throes of an Ogam orgy. Everyone is convinced that the markings on the rocks are Ogam. Driving down to Derry yesterday, I saw Lucy and Mary crawling along on their hands and knees examining the stone wall around Herb's field. They looked like a couple of sheep."

"How crazy. Why Herb's wall?"

"The new idea is that many of these caves—excuse me, chambers—were accepted by the early settlers as root cellars built by earlier settlers. Probably didn't give them much thought at all. They were just grateful to find a bunch of rocks they didn't have to pry out of the earth and they used them in their stone walls. Charlie Reed is the high priest of archeology in Lofton now, and Barry Fell's book, 'America B.C.' is his bible.

"Walter, Terry and Kay have serious differences of opinion as to where the temple should be recreated. Actually, that will be for you to say, Tish, if Heman decrees that the land is yours."

When Hilary paused for a drink, I asked the question that had been haunting me all week.

"What about Lew Weber?"

"What about him, Tish? He must have gone about his business and I daresay you won't hear from him. Why don't you put him out of your mind?"

"Reason would have me do that but Hil, I just can't. I saw Lew—you didn't. He's a decent young man." I told Hilary about Lew, his brother and his grandmother visiting Lofton years ago. "I make my living looking at faces. I don't think I'm wrong about him. I feel in my bones, my guts, my heart that he's here in Lofton and that he's in trouble and I'm going to find him."

"But how, Tish? The law can't help you and I don't think The Marshal will welcome you."

"I'm not sure yet but I am sure I can't live with myself if I don't try. You can help, Hilary—will you?"

He shrugged, smiling. "You know I will. More fool I."

He was appalled at what I asked him to do.

6

The annual Labor Day fair was given by and for Lofton's volunteer fire department. Kay said it was more like a yard sale than a fair but I heard her say she wouldn't miss it for the world. Hilary called it the Lofton lard sale, claiming that all the baked goods were made with lard. That wasn't quite true—a few good cooks really knocked themselves out. There was always a dash for Lucy's table and in two seconds her entire supply of brownies disappeared. Her secret ingredient was Rice Krispies. Another neighbor baked a rum cake that made me swoon. My other imperative was Herb's wife, Sarah's, beach plum jelly made from last year's harvest. Only a long spell of life below the poverty level would make me sell anything so precious.

Whatever happened to homemade doughnuts? I faded back in time and caught that delicious smell and could taste that first bite of deep fried crust. After tearing myself away from a vision of doughnuts cooling in an enamel colander, I automatically licked my fingers. And baked beans. They'd been absent from kitchen bazaars for a couple of decades. Oh, the penalties of the era of physical fitness. I should be jogging instead of dreaming about doughnuts and baked beans.

Scarlett O'Hara's front porch was the geographic

center of the fair. Great piles of pots and pans testified to the fact that she had less and less time to cook and, as Marge observed, fewer mouths to feed. Scarlett had arrived in Lofton about five years ago, a widow with two boys old enough now to be off on their own this summer.

I laughed at the collectibles sign under the trestle table which held the dark and dented cookware. Scarlett's intimate contact with the Blarney stone seemed to give her license to pass off all her old props as examples of fine old Irish glass, china, linen or whatever. When asked about the origin of her name, Scarlett burst into song—"It was Mary, Mary, long before the fashions changed—oh, it's a grand old name." Forget Tara. Her glorious hair was clearly the reason for her nickname.

Curious about her fainting spell after the explosion. I was sorry to see someone else standing arms akimbo behind the display of pots and pans. In another way, I was glad she wasn't there. It might be easier to accomplish my mission.

Nearby, Kay was trying to come to a decision. Should she buy Mrs. Blount's pot holders shaped like ducks or like cows? I was enchanted by the stunning man offering her advice about this important choice.

Walter Upson had shaved off his beard. The remaining mustache, in scale with his size, was handsomely trimmed and his chestnut locks had been tended by someone more adept than his last barber.

Kay was obviously taking a new look at my secret passion. She had to back up a few paces to focus on the total man. Walter's professional pruning was probably inspired by her actions the other night at the inn when she handed him a napkin to trap a blob of lobster butter on his beard.

Roaming around aimlessly, I was suddenly confronted by three Ringers, the young woman from the battlefield and the two warriors. They looked right at me and smiled. Never having seen a Ringer smile, for an instant I thought they were going to bite me. I backed up and bumped into Kay who offered to share her salted almonds.

"That's a surprise." She bared her teeth in a false smile, imitating the Ringers. "Are they mending fences?"

"It's my guess," Walter said, "that they realize the explosion bombed."

"We'll excuse you, Walter," Kay laughed. "But seriously, it would be fatal for them if the town were really up in arms. Couldn't you all run them out?"

"Not unless they break the law. Even then it would be tricky. They do legally own Amber Trees and the farms. If someone had been injured at the explosion, that might be a different matter."

I asked Walter, "I've been out of it all week. Weren't there some noisy repercussions afterwards?"

"Half the town's on an archeological hunt and lots of others are tightlipped and angry, but I haven't heard about any plots or plans. This isn't the kind of publicity we want for the area so I've been trying to keep the lid on any overt action. Any news of the kid, Tish?"

I shook my head. I didn't want to talk about Lew. "I'm going to find him."

"I'll be damned." Walter hadn't heard me. I followed him to a stack of baled hay at the edge of the town green.

Sam Loon, a taciturn local farmer, had a popular product for sale. Annually, he sold bundled hay needed to bed down gardens and to insulate old stone foundations.

"How would you like to paint him, Tish?" Kay nodded toward Farmer Loon. I said emphatically no. I loathed the man and remarked that Sam's pasty round face wasn't helped by eyes like frozen peas.

"And in the produce department," Kay added, "his ears looked like huge dried apricots."

Walter whispered behind us. "His fingers look like bratwurst."

"His nose," Kay said, "looks like a Jerusalem artichoke."

I no longer heard their grocery list. I was mesmerized by the object Sam was dusting with his cap. The bales of hay were arranged in U-shape to frame his archeological treasure.

Suffused with mixed feelings, I stared at the stone and said nothing.

Loon handed me a clipboard with a captive pencil on a string.

"Silent sale," he said.

For a moment I thought he said setting sail. I looked at the list of names on the legal yellow sheet. Most of the names were of villagers. Beside each name under a column marked with a dollar sign were the prices offered by the silent bidder. The last entry was forty dollars. For Loon's stone? My stone? Stunned, I wondered if forty dollars was high or low and who did Loon think he was selling a stone that probably belonged to me? Hilary told me that after the explosion people had taken away most of the portable marked stones. Was all this archeological talk nonsense? Where was Charlie, my expert? I had so many questions. Where was the archaeologist the governor had promised to send down?

My week's retreat at home suddenly seemed inadequate. I wanted to scream, or cry, or, worse, hit Loon's avaricious face.

I turned away. Diversions and a wandering mind could be my enemy today. I must concentrate. I owed it to Hilary to do my part. Lord knows I was asking a lot of him.

Scarlett called me and I withdrew from the distasteful encounter with Sam Loon. Unable to park in her own driveway, she made her way toward me around tables of aprons and cakes. I hoped my smile hid my anxiety.

Hilary's description of Scarlett as a dish was probably inspired by her ample bust, her wasp waist, and her flirtatious manner, but we all admired her as a capable and conscientious business woman.

Normally, elbows bent, her hands dangled from her wrists like a poodle begging. I was always tempted to yank them down or shake one. She conducted conversations like the leader of a symphony. Scarlett required five square feet to express a simple declarative sentence. Her hands waved through the air describing shapes and sizes and her elbows were wings. It was advisable to stand back when she was talking about anything larger than the minimum building lot. Today her arms were folded close to her body.

We expressed our concern for each other and denied being regular fainters.

"Those bastards," I said, referring of course to the Ringers.

"Oh, don't say that, Tish. I'm sure the explosion was a terrible mistake. I don't think they intended to blow up the chamber. You're judging them harshly. They're perfectly nice people."

"Nice! I haven't even had a word of apology for blowing up the chamber and it's probably mine. I too would like to think well of them but certainly behavior like that doesn't invite tolerance."

A gray stretch limousine with darkened windows drove down Main Street. It attracted little attention. We were used to seeing those hearse-like horrors. The car turned in the gates at Amber Trees.

A young boy standing near us comments, "There go the hop heads."

Scarlett scolded him. "Now don't you talk that way. You don't know anything about those people."

"Oh come on, Mrs. O'Hara," his companion said. "You know that limousine is full of submachine guns."

"And bombs," the other boy added.

Scarlett shook her head. "Tish, we must learn to live with them."

"Do you really think that just by wishing you can turn a cult like that into good neighbors, good citizens? What do we have in common? Nothing— except we all live here."

Scarlett always liked to serve up her clients. She had cocktail parties for her new homeowners. She made an effort to introduce them to compatible people. But I felt she was misguided in her enthusiasm for the Ringers. The possibility of being chummy with them seemed remote. The Ringers as a social problem didn't really concern me. I was frightened, not just for Lew Weber, but for all of us. I couldn't share Scarlett's complacency. My viscera were responding in ways I couldn't ignore. Destructive cults were moving into rural areas all over the country. I sensed the potential for a really dangerous conflict. None of us had faced up to the possibility that these intruders might intend to devour Lofton. That the townspeople would be forced out, not the newcomers. None of us knew what the Ringers believed. Yet Scarlett thought they were benign.

How do you blow up something by mistake? You don't. Why would you wear a fake beard except to deceive, though Charlie told me that the use of beards figured in Druid practices. But certainly the Ringers weren't Druids. Or were they? Self-appointed priests believing what?

Yes, I was frightened. What a fool I was to consider invading the Ring of Right to find a young man I had known for ten minutes. But I knew I must.

Farmer Loon's marked stone riveted Scarlett's attention. Without even looking at him, she held out her hand for the clipboard and added her name to the list. I couldn't see the amount she wrote down under the dollar column.

She pulled my arm. "Come in and have some iced tea with me, Tish, or a drink."

From the height of her front steps, I looked around for Hilary and, catching his attention, tapped my wrist watch. He responded by holding up one hand, fingers spread apart. Five o'clock. Then with a crooked smile he raised his thumb. I returned the gesture.

Following Scarlett I stood in the kitchen doorway while she poured tea from a pitcher on the counter, adding a handful of ice cubes and a sprig of mint. It made me realize how parched and weary I was.

"Are you really going to pay fifty or sixty dollars for that stone?" I asked.

We sat outside on the back porch which overlooked Clement Hollow. A green-on-green tapestry unrolled up to Stratton Mountain, its dark shape marked with pale green ski trails, the veins of a giant industry.

"My father was a Druid." Scarlett smiled at my quizzical expression, "though he was really more of a leprechaun." Just the mention of her father brought forth the hint of a brogue. "At least he thought he was a Druid and we were brought up surrounded by the props and trappings of would-be Druids.

"We? Do you still have family in Ireland?"

"No, it was just me and my sister, Judith. She died three years ago. She held more to the old ways. I put it all behind me when I married O'Hara and came to America. But this sudden business of discovering Druid temples! And destroying one is very unsettling."

"Tell me about your father. How could he be a Druid?"

"There are Druid societies all over England and Ireland. Most of them are an excuse for the men to meet and drink themselves silly. Too, it's an ancient custom for Celts to worship horse racing. You can see that it all adds up to fun for the fellows. Some groups take their Druidic meetings quite seriously. Certainly my father did. Astronomy was at the heart of his interests and he and his friends always met at a small observatory built on a high tor behind the farm on the burren."

"The burren?"

"Our part of County Clare is paved with limestone—miles and miles of flat rocks, mountains covered with flat rocks. You've got to see it, Tish, on a gray day, it's grim and ominous. In the sunshine my father called it a walkway to heaven. Here and there you find Druid temples."

"Do they look like caves, or, I should say, chambers?"

"More like horse sheds. Two or three upright stone walls with a huge slab or two for a roof on top." Her hands formed the shape.

"Are they protected?"

She smiled. "By cows or maybe a bunch of sheep. Of course, in Ireland the Georgian Society keeps an eye on all monuments and ruins. When you hike over the burren and come upon a stone temple, believe me, you feel at one with the ancient Druids."

"Do you really believe it was a Druid temple the Ringers blew up?"

"You bet I do. My father told me I'd find temples in the States. He always said he'd like to come over here and stake out New Ireland and proclaim it the Land of the Druids." She shook her head. "A little crazy, I guess, but it was hard not to believe him. We've got to get that rock from greedy Sam Loon. Walter and Terry are trying to track down the other stones. Maybe I'll ask the congregation. Possibly some of them don't know how important it is to return the stones." Scarlett was optimistic.

"Probably the Ringers have rocks slathered with cement and set in a wall by now. If you all really want to reconstruct the thing you'd better hurry because . . . " I didn't finish my sentence. My watch alarm was set to buzz two minutes before five. At the sound of it I jumped to my feet. "Thanks, dear, gotta go." I made a staggered run around and among Scarlett's sea of overstuffed furniture and came to a stop on the porch behind the long table of pots and pans.

Sun glinted from Hilary's spectacles. Even at a distance I could see the relief on his face when he saw me. I raised my thumb.

Hilary stood in front of eight men and two women, members of the volunteer fire department. He stood behind a card table. With a large wooden fork he stirred the contents of a wicker basket.

Every year I vowed it was the last time I would volunteer to do a portrait of the raffle winner. Every year I weakened. This time I really dreaded the outcome.

As the founder of the volunteer fire department, Hilary was its honorary chief and always presided at the annual fair. He folded his tall thin frame to speak to a tiny blond toddler who had been chosen to pick this year's winning ticket. With elaborate showmanship and a barker's spiel he lifted the little girl up in the air and aimed her head first into the basket. She squealed with excitement.

She plunged he hand into the basket to retrieve the winning number. That was our prearranged signal. Poised and prepared for action I gave it my best effort. With a wild crash, Scarlett's table of pots and pans and assorted junk cascaded down the porch steps, bouncing and rolling in every direction. When the din subsided Hilary could be heard.

"We've got it, ladies and gentlemen, we've got a winner," he said, waving the white ticket stub overhead. "Once again a winner, folks. The fire department is the winner and so is the person whose name is on this ticket." When he gained everyone's attention, he handed the paper to Herb. "You tell 'em, Herb."

In the silence, Herb looked at the stub, shook his head and handed it back to Hilary. "The winner is, ladies and gentlemen, the winner is one of the new members of our community—Alan Smith."

When I hugged Hilary later, he admitted he'd been scared.

"How mortifying to be caught cheating. God, I can't imagine anything worse."

He held out his arm, the palm of his hand facing me. "Empty, right?"

"Right."

A deft movement produced a silver half dollar. "Now you see it", he caused it to vanish, "now you don't. Nothing like a third rate magician to get you in trouble, Tish. Are you really going to paint that creature?"

"You bet I am and I'm going to take a good look around Amber Trees. Maybe The Marshal will even show me around himself then at least I'll know where Lew isn't."

Hilary assumed his adjudicating pose in the wing chair. Long legs stuck out and crossed at the ankle, elbows on the arms and his hands in a steeple under his chin. I could imagine his long figure sliding out of the chair and onto a sarcophagus like the Elizabethan dramatist he resembled.

"Charlie doesn't believe that Lew Weber exists, and even though you think of him as a dear boy, he is the law in our neck of the woods."

Hilary waved me to silence. "Of course, of course he believes you, Tish. He thinks you're wonderful, But he needs hard evidence. He thinks there's a possibility he appeared and went on his way—but that perhaps your fall confused your recollections."

More of that talk was all I needed to make my head ache. With more thanks I said goodbye to Hilary and went in the kitchen to brew some tea. I had a tough decision to make. How many brownies should I freeze and how many should I eat.

7

The next day when I pulled my red cashmere cardigan out of the dresser drawer another piece of red caught my eye. I knelt down gingerly and reached under and retrieved the plastic bag holding Lew Weber's kerchief.

Promptly I dialed Charlie. A bloodhound, he explained, could only be used if the police were searching for a missing person and they had no such evidence about Lew Weber. In fact, they had no evidence that he even existed.

I knew what he thought, but I persisted. "The Department of Motor Vehicles. Have you tried them? Have you checked the license bureau?"

"Last week, Mrs. McWhinny. There is no Lew Weber, no driver's license nor is there a car registered in his name in Vermont.

"Did you check under the name of Teddy, probably Theodore or Edward?" He hadn't done that. How about Lew's grandmother? Yes, he had asked Terry to look through old Inn books but Terry hadn't found any Weber which, Charlie said, probably wasn't Grandma's name anyhow. Give it some time, he advised, and the usual parting shot—forget him.

Disappointed, I considered looking up bloodhound in the Yellow Pages when I thought of Clyde Razor. He had bloodhounds, or one at least, that I'd seen tied outside the door of this tarpaper shack on the hill road to Chester. Clyde didn't answer his phone. Then I remembered someone told me he only answered the phone on Sunday morning. He had the instrument installed at the insistence of this daughter who lived in New Hampshire and called him on Sundays. Clyde regarded it as a nuisance. I whistled for Lulu and climbed in the station wagon. It would do her good to meet a real working dog.

Clyde was stacking wood. St. Clyde, I thought, because he had a halo around his head, a pulsating halo of tiny insects. The bloodhound bayed. Lulu barked. When the cacophony subsided, I explained my visit to Clyde. He maneuvered the cigar butt to the other side of his mouth.

"Can't help you, Letitia. You know these critters have to be trained."

My heart sank. "You mean he isn't a real bloodhound? He can't follow a scent?"

He gathered a handful of loose skin around the hound's neck and gave it an affectionate squeeze.

"She's out of practice. Aren't you, Cootie?"

"She has to practice?" I was amazed.

"Sure. How old's the scent you want tracked?"

"A little over a week."

"Well, she can track your party if the tracks aren't more than two weeks old. That is, if I train her for a few days. She's out of the habit. She'd just think we was playing if I gave her something to smell right now. I'd have to charge you, you know. I've got to practice her every morning and every afternoon for four days at least."

"I'll pay, Clyde, I'll pay. Can you start right now? Can she practice this afternoon? I've got to find this young man."

67

"Sure, sure. Keep your shirt on." He looked at his watch. "It's Tuesday. I could come see you, say, Sunday morning and we'll see what we can do for you."

I'd never heard of a bloodhound practicing but then I didn't know much about bloodhounds except that they were one of the oldest breeds of dog and that their testimony was allowed in court. Clyde explained to me that the unfortunate thing about using a bloodhound was that they were usually called to follow the trail too late, after all else had failed and the tracks had been destroyed by earlier searchers. The bloodhounds used by the police were trained every day, he said, rain or shine.

I had to be content with what Clyde offered. At least there was a glimmer of hope. Would Cootie's raunchy odor make it impossible, I wondered, for her to smell anything beyond her own aura. I locked Lew's kerchief in the glove compartment and turned toward Londonderry.

In front of the IGA grocery store I locked the car, and left Lulu peeking through a crack in the window. I felt responsible for my cargo which was a trash bag full of money. Seeing it, any Vermonter would assume I was on my way to the dump even though my load was unusually tidy for my weekly trip. But some mean-spirited person might realize I was transporting money from the fair en route to the Bellows Falls Trust and try to steal the loot. You can be sure the volunteer firemen hadn't handed me the total proceeds from the fair, which I'm sure was neatly packed, stacked, labeled and secured with rubber bands. The money I had to deposit had been personally fluffed up by Lucy and Hank, who said the bag should look huge. The crumpled bills were the money raised by the portrait raffle, and the Londonderry newspaper had suggested we make a newsworthy occasion of depositing it. The event was set for 12 noon, and the editor said she would be taking the pictures herself.

After some unexciting marketing—bananas, dog food, detergent and the like—I checked my watch and it was time for my engagement with the press.

I left Lulu in the car and in view of what happened it was a wise move. I walked up to the bank with the bag of bills slung over my shoulder, like Santa Claus. I waved at Wendy Holt. She held a light meter at arm's length, directed at the door of the bank. Wendy's pigtails made her look like a chubby 12-year-old but Hilary had told me she had long since earned her master's degree in journalism and was also a crackerjack photographer.

The heavy bank door opened. I stepped quickly backwards to avoid being knocked over by a couple of men who appeared to be emerging from the bank backwards. Motorcyclists, was my first thought. They both wore black leather jackets.

"Hey, what goes on?" Wendy yelled.

Speechless, I looked at the two men. They turned around and one pointed a machine gun toward us. I slowly lowered the bag of money over my shoulder, holding it in front of me. Both bandits wore ski masks. The smaller figure stared at me with eyes that had a gender. They were a woman's eyes. She pulled two canvas bags from the bank and across the sidewalk and threw them into a dark blue pickup.

When the armed bandit swung around to dash toward the truck, the nose of his machine gun caught in the loop of lavender yarn tied at the throat of my trash bag. An extra yank threw the bag overhead and a blizzard of crumpled bills cascaded over the bank robbers, over Wendy Holt and over me, and fluttered onto the sidewalk. Some landed in the pickup. A Vermont zephyr distributed the rest around the parking lot.

Amid the floating bills the armed bandit paused in apparent indecision. His companion started the pickup and yelled, "Come on, for Christ's sake, come on." Both inside the truck, they backed out of the parking space and crashed into the side of an Idlenot dairy truck. Then, spurting forward, they made a U-turn and headed for the South Derry exit. Before I could catch my breath, a woman stepped out of the hairdressing shop right behind me and knocked me off balance. I landed painfully on my knees, thigh-deep in one, five, ten and twenty dollar bills.

She said "I'm sorry" five times between knocking me down and jumping into her dark blue pickup. She too shot out of the parking space backwards and just missed the dented white truck. She drove out of the lot in the opposite direction from the way the robbers had gone.

It wasn't my ears ringing, it was a police siren I'd been hearing. I rose to my feet in time to see a police car, sirens screaming, following the wrong blue pickup. A second police car squealed to a stop in front of us and before I could even greet the officer who ran towards me, he roughly twisted me around and held my arms behind me.

"My ribs," I howled. "My ribs. Let go."

The bank manager rushed out, his usually pink face was white.

"Mrs. McWhinny! How could you?"

Perhaps I should be flattered that the manager thought I was the mastermind of a successful bank

70

heist but my ribs hurt too much to view the events and the present scene with objectivity.

"Tell him to let go of me," I snarled.

Wendy saved me from offering a selection of obscenities I was ready to deliver. "Let her go." She touched the officer's hand. "This is money from the Lofton fair. It has nothing to do with the robbery. They went thataway." She pointed west.

We were collecting quite a crowd. A friend of mine, her head screwed up in the paraphernalia of a permanent wave, took my arm and handed me a cup of coffee. I couldn't hold it. Hilary elbowed his way to my side. He was beaming.

"When the gang sent you off to deposit the money, Tish, we didn't really expect you to rob the bank. I know they'd like to thank you for trying, but it's beyond the call of ... "

"Oh, shut up, Hil, and get me out of here."

"Wendy's going to win the Pulitzer prize for photo journalism. What a stunning coup," he laughed. "Why this has to be the most completely photographed bank robbery in history."

Wendy came over, removing a film from her camera. "Wasn't it wonderful, Mrs. McWhinny? Today has been the highlight of my short undistinguished career. Imagine photographing bank robbers! And you were wonderful, too. Did the one with the gun say anything to you?" She flipped open her notebook.

I shook my head. But the eyes ...

Escape for me was impossible. The star quality of my performance had enchanted my public. Bank employees and other eager helpers were stuffing bills into baskets, bags and pockets. After a hopeless, brief interview with the police officer, I was propelled down the sidewalk by my fans to the Idlenot Dairy restaurant where the consensus was that I needed food. That seemed silly to me.

"It's not," I protested to Hilary when we sat down, "as though the bandits had stolen my peanut butter sandwich," and "No," I assured Wendy, "while those eyes looked familiar, I didn't recognize the person behind them."

"I think it was a woman," she said. "In fact, I'm sure it was."

I couldn't seem to think of any woman I knew who would be robbing a bank.

"How about a female Ringer?" Wendy asked.

I don't really approve of ordering greasy french fried potatoes, so I pondered as I dunked a couple of Hilary's fries in ketchup. The only female Ringer with whom I had locked eyes was the angry woman at the battle scene in front of the chamber. I'd have to put that masked face in the back of my mind to jell. They were the light eyes of a malamute.

The Idlenot truck driver came over to our booth and asked me to sign a paper stating that I had witnessed the accident. He joined us for coffee and a detailed review of the thrilling heist.

"Wait till it hits the papers—everyone's going to want to feel my dent. Imagine, bank robbers! And the police chasing the *wrong* truck!"

The only reason I could endure the week waiting for Cootie Razor to practice was that my portrait model, The Marshal, was out of town. I persuaded Kay to further postpone my portrait work so that I could fully recuperate. I asked Hilary to field any questions or problems that concerned the chamber's site.

Heman Chase, after sprinting around with his tripod and compass and hundred-foot tape, made calculations on a collapsible, portable desk of his own invention and announced that my property line went right through the center of what was left of the Druid temple.

Convinced that Lew was held captive by the Ringers, time wasted—more than a week—made me sick with anxiety. Maybe he'd gone to camp up on the mountain. But without oreos? I doubted it.

Unrolling a heavy Hudson Bay blanket on the floor, I resolved to bring my being into a state of serenity. For me the entrance to this refreshingly vacant realm was the head stand. With my feet elevated, I could imagine my brain was undulating. Soon, after long controlled exhalations, I could feel my body slowly being suffused with ripples of energy. Ideally, one then achieves the beta state which finds the rational intellectual mind at work. But I must have skipped some part of the exercise because once again, relaxed on the blanket, the same old refrain echoed in my head. Lew Weber. You've got to find Lew Weber.

I sat up quickly. If painting the Marshal's portrait didn't further my search and if Cootie Razor's nose led me nowhere, there was another way.

Kay answered her phone right away. Yes, I was correct, she had an appointment with her back doctor Wednesday. Dr. Femur's office was in Boston. Yes, she'd love to take me for my seasonal visit to Johnson's, my favorite art supply store. Yes. she'd be glad to drive my comfortable big station wagon so my ribs wouldn't come unglued. She welcomed the opportunity to leave her car at the shop in Brattle-boro. Kay's car, in my opinion, accounted for her back troubles. Kind Hilary would look after Lulu. He was convinced she liked chamber music. He also liked to cook when Lulu visited—said he liked having a happy little garbage pail. I certainly couldn't tell him the real purpose of my trip to Boston.

Walter called. When I told him about going to Boston with Kay he offered to be our chauffeur. When I refused his offer, I probably did Kay out of a delicious lunch at the Ritz or Locke's but I didn't want to be part of a social event. I had to attend to business.

8

Once out of the tunnel at Copley Square we turned over to Beacon Street where Kay let me out at the Hampshire House. We arranged to meet there late in the afternoon. From there I walked up to Johnson's on Newbury Street and spent almost an hour buying art supplies, canvases, varnishes and some new brushes. What size portrait would the Marshal want? His prize entitled him to nothing more than a small charcoal or pencil sketch but I intended to paint him from toe to toupee if it would give me an opportunity to search the place. I paused, rubbing a camel's hair brush on my cheek. Maybe the old stinker would insist on posing in my studio. Well, I'd handle that when the time came.

I trudged back looking like a peasant going to market. A helpful bus boy stowed my wares behind a bulge in the Hampshire House lobby.

Settled in a comfortable leather armchair in the bar I looked up at the chin-whiskers of a magnificent moose who, with his twin, looked down over the agreeable room. I ordered dry sherry on the rocks and asked for the yellow pages.

Under "wigs" in the heavy book there were twenty-two entries. Reading the ads I realized that most of them catered to those who had lost their hair because of chemotherapy or for other medical reasons. I certainly didn't want to get involved in some serious transaction to buy a wig for a one-night stand. Under "theatrical supplies", there were a handful of names of those who sold wigs, some of them nearby. I leaned back and thought about this next errand, my real reason for coming to Boston.

If Cootie fails me and I'm locked in with the Marshal and unable to explore the house, my only other chance to find Lew was to use a disguise and simply infiltrate the place. Once I would have been terrified at the idea of such a risky adventure. But two years ago a brush with death in a car accident, surgery, traction and other frightening indignities had made me feel less than immortal. It made me realize what a frail gift life is and that it was silly to weigh the odds of survival because survival will probably be taken out of one's hands in any event. I was convinced that Lew Weber was being held by the Ringers and the fact that no one believed me no longer mattered to me. Too, it was intensely irritating to be treated like an irrational being. Even if I did take someone into my confidence, tell Kay or Hilary of my intentions, what could they do to help? Nothing—except possibly notify my relatives that I'd bought it—or vanished.

The waiter arranged a chicken sandwich and coffee on the marble-top table. A fine room for street watching, I was astonished at the masses of young people, probably arriving to fill the groves of Academe, which spread daily along Beacon Street. My eyes went over their heads to the Common. A few leaves had turned which gave me a twinge. The beginning of the last act of summer. I wondered if it would be mine, too. In spite of considering myself fearless, I didn't want this harebrained scheme to be my last solo show.

On my way to the theatrical section of town beyond the Common, I came upon Jack's Joke Store and saw wigs hanging in the window. I guess it was Jack himself who greeted me cheerfully.

"So what does it look like to you? A joke store? Well, you know, that's just what it is."

He then silently observed me as I inspected his highly organized madhouse. How miserable for genial Jack to be obliged to wait on a solemn jokester. He held a mirror for me so I could decide on the appropriate wig and dispensed helpful advice as I chose a shoulder-length blond number. I looked like an aged Swedish actress clinging to her youth with peroxide. The wig hid my frizzy gray hair and, very important to me, it felt secure. Mine was not the kind of an act that would allow for a comic routine of a wig removed by the branch of a potted plant or blown aloft by a breeze.

I examined Jack's collection of zany eyeglasses but remembered that I had a small round wire-rimmed pair at home. There were spook costumes hanging on the wall that looked rather like Ringer robes but I had a bolt of plain monkscloth in the studio that I used as a backdrop for sitters. Would Hilary laugh if I brought him a monster mask? Suddenly I had to hold on to the counter—I felt almost sick at the thought of what I planned. It isn't a joke, you old fool. Not a time for monster masks and exploding cigars.

Jack looked over his half glasses as he handed me change from twenty dollars.

"You okay, lady?"

I nodded.

"Hope it's a good party."

With my hand on the doorknob I contained a tremendous urge to throw my wig onto the counter and forget the whole damn thing. Through the glass door I caught sight of Kay across the street. Her honey hair cought the sunlight like a halo. Opening the door I called.

"Kay, hey, over here." I watched Kay duck behind a mail truck. "Kay."

She had seen me. Our eyes had met. I felt as though a fist had hit my chest. Standing there on Park Square my arm still raised in greeting, I backed up a few steps and leaned against the joke store window. My eyes were riveted on the mail truck. It moved down the street. Kay was nowhere in sight.

Was she following me? What could Kay possibly be doing that she wanted to hide from me? Dismayed, I sagged against the window.

"I'm worried about you, lady." Jack looked around the door. "Want me to call a taxi?"

"No, no thank you." How long had I been standing there? "I thought I saw a friend."

"A friend? More like a ghost, I'd say." The pressure of his hand on my elbow ended my state of shock. Thanking him, I crossed into the Common. Could it have been someone who looked like Kay? I rejected that. My eyes were too sharp to make a mistake like that. I felt profoundly hurt. It was deceit that always hurt the most. But why was Kay deceiving me?

I usually loved going to The Bookstore on Chestnut Street but Kay had spoiled it for me today. I bought for myself a copy of "America B.C.".

Browsing around a favorite market on Church Street I reflected how in past years I would have bought all kinds of exotic food to take back to Lofton: great cheese, pasta, huge capers, flat bread. Now, every delicacy was available in Vermont, even the Village store across the street did a lively business in products like caviar and macadamia nuts. They sold three kinds of smoked salmon. I bought a sinful looking chocolate and sponge cake roll to share with Hilary and for the ride home I bought a dozen twisted cheese straws.

It was too early to meet for the trip home so I roamed aimlessly around the Back Bay on streets I knew, looking at houses I didn't see. In the Public Garden, I sat on a bench until I saw the station wagon roll up to the entrance of Hampshire House.

Kay was full of talk about artists she had visited during the day. One, she said, made bas-reliefs of chrome-plated pasta. Another for whom she expressed concern was a young woman who wrapped branches of trees in ace bandages.

"What else did you do?" I asked.

"Aside from the usual appointment with Femur, nothing. Lunch with a friend at Florian's. It was lovely outside watching the people go by. And I wore a sweater down here today! My Lord, it's like the middle of August." She prattled on. "And I caught the new show at the Vose. Stopped at Shreve's to get a wedding present for Bettina. The tiniest salt and pepper shakers in captivity. And that's about it. How about you?

I didn't mention Jack's Joke Shop. If Kay noticed the joke shop bag in the back of the wagon, she didn't mention it. Why didn't I ask her? What were you doing spying on me? Why were you hiding from me? Why didn't I say, "Kay, you saw me. What goes on? Tell me." Why didn't I ask her what she was doing on Park Square? I opened and closed my mouth a few times but nothing came out. I put my hand up to feel the dagger in my heart.

Kay caught me examining her profile as she fiddled with the radio. She felt her cheek. "Something wrong with my face?"

I shook my head and leaned back. I hoped my eyelids would contain the bitter tears that were forming. I felt used.

Kay patted my knee. "Good. You take a nap. There's not much traffic. We'll be home in no time."

After a silent lecture on mind controls I tried meditation which, contrary to Webster's definition, is a total absence of thought. Any mental image or thought is observed with detachment, while like a small cloud it passes across the screen of your mind. The emptiness of that screen is the measure of your mental achievment. Kay was too close and I was too upset to enter that refreshing state of serenity. But just the effort of concentrating on something other than my hurt feelings pulled me at least part way out of my morass.

Kay offered me a Lifesaver. "What do you think of Walter sans beard?"

"He'd do well on Mount Rushmore. A great profile."

"Lord, all that hair. I feel this is the first time I've ever seen the guy. I hate that moist pink-lipped look most beavers have."

"How does he stack up against Terry?" A nosy question but Kay clearly wanted to talk about Walter. She took her hands off the wheel and spread them wide.

"Like fifty miles apart. Terry is so complete, in control, so good at everything, smooth. I must say, he seems distressingly immune to my charms. I'd say Walter even without his beard is a bull. Charging into things unaware of the noise he makes." She laughed. "Know what he does for kicks?"

I didn't.

"He's painting stars on all the ceiling in his house. The Andromeda room, the Pleiades room and so forth. He's really excited about the chamber. Says he's prepared to believe ours is a temple to the goddess Bel and he's been studying the possible celestial orientation of the one you fell into." She looked at me. "You don't seem to be in the spirit of Lofton's archeological spree, Tish."

"You know why I'm depressed, dear. I've got to find that young man—Lew Weber. If you could have seen him, Kay. If Hilary had seen him. If anyone had seen him. Sweet Charlie thinks I'm addlepated. Even Hil doubts me. But I'm going to find him."

"I've seen that bulldog look on your face before. Will you let me help, Tish?"

"Not now. Not yet." This sounded like my dear young friend. Why had she avoided me on the corner of Park Square?

Before I could fall back into perplexity and depression, it was time to drop Kay at the repair shop in Brattleboro where her car was being fixed. Sliding behind the wheel, I watched her pick her way around barrels and tires and disappear into the garage. I wondered if time would tell me about Kay's behavior in Boston.

Propped up against my front door in Lofton was the Rutland Herald. Attached to it a note written in Hilary's bold hand—"Ah, fame. Looks like a press release for a Hepburn film."

Lulu showered me with her effusive version of

love. I kicked off my city shoes and dumped the packages from Johnson's in the studio. I shoved the wig into a bureau drawer. With a mug of tea laced with rum I settled down to read the paper.

The two-inch headline made me laugh out loud. "Lofton Artist Showers Bandits With Bills". The pictures beneath were spectacular. It was gratifying that Wendy Holt's name was prominent along the bottom. My face appeared wreathed in fluttering bills. I gasped at the inch between the bandit's gun and my belt buckle. Another testimony to Wendy's skill was a comical record of the exact moment of impact between the pick-up and the Idlenot truck. Seen through the windshield, the masked robbers looked like twins with their mouths open in surprise.

The story continued, saying that the police thought the heist had been engineered by robbers who were acquainted with the area, because that particular day was a time for payroll deliveries to accommodate local industries. The Ringers weren't mentioned.

"Letitia McWhinny, prominent Vermont artist, clad in blue jeans, a bush jacket and a straw hat, looked like a mad Lady Bountiful distributing money to a couple of Halloween toughs."

The paper fell to the floor. Warming my hands around the china mug, I wished for Doug. Life with him seemed a million years ago. How he would have loved the bank heist. The hell with wishing. I knew better than to indulge myself in such a simple-minded activity. I missed Doug in more ways than one. I'd had a couple of lukewarm affairs since he died, leaving my emotions untouched. I loved Hil but he was more brother than beau. Maybe that was why he loved me, too. I made no demands on him, certainly not on his manhood. I had a feeling he'd retired that part of his life years ago. Parts of me seemed to be in the cooler but nothing had been wrapped in mothballs. I hadn't surrended my gender to elderly androgeny, but I had to admit the facade was getting kind of crinkly.

Doug wouldn't have approved of my dangerous manhunt. He would have been appalled at the amateurish trick Hilary had performed at my request. What if some sharp observer had seen his sleight-of-hand. Distaste for myself made me shudder—even as I planned my next foray.

9

Good Lord, what was it? The Maginot Line, that grim barricade built to prevent the Germans from invading France before the last World War? What first appeared to be a wall was a carefully stacked pile of rocks rather like a shepherd's tower, some pale and smooth reminiscent of marble, others dark and obviously pried from recent intimate contact with earth. A few were light gray, what I call Vermont rocks, covered with sage green lichen and moss.

The rough monument took time and effort and, I guess, speed (it hadn't been there three days ago) and was impressive. Unable to see over the top of it, I maneuvered around to see what was on the other side.

A few scattered rocks on the bottom of the dory-size earthen pit were all that was left of my Druid temple.

I reached out to touch what seemed to be an inscription on the topmost rock. The pressure of my hand sent the cone of the rock pile tumbling and once again I made an unplanned descent into the temple. I slid backwards with my hands raking the crumbling earth for support while Lulu scrambled beside me. Had the pile of rocks fallen in our direction, the Druid temple would have become my grave. A few big rocks stopped at the rim of the pit while the others tolled toward other points of the compass.

I felt my head. It was intact. I flexed my muscles and wiggled my fingers and toes. Lulu was fine. She was cautiously sniffing at the disturbed bugs. Unhurt, I expanded my lungs and vented my feelings by loudly calling the Ringers every insulting and vulgar name in the book. Why had those horrible people taken so much trouble with their creation? Was it symbolic? Were they tidying up? Was it supposed to fall on the curious? I had heard that any effort of the Marshall amounted to overkill. Was this his idea or the work of his bird-brained zealot yardman?

Emptying my sneakers, I took a look around me. A pale slab of rock caught my eye. I don't know what intuition made me turn it over. Its smooth under-surface was inscribed. It didn't require the expertise of an archeologist to realize that the characters had not been incised eons ago by Celts or even centuries ago by Indians. The scratched letters looked as though they had been made yesterday.

I licked my finger and rubbed the lines. Pumice stuck to the swirls of my fingerprint told me the message was new. Was it in Ogam? Twisting the stone around did nothing to enlighten me.

Trying to figure out how to lug home my provocative find, I stood up and pulled off my belt, which I thought might be a helpful tool. Then I saw the fence. Its upright rods had been driven into the ground on the Ringers' side of the pit. Clearly they were saying the hell with the rocks, but people, keep out.

Lulu barked and ran toward a figure emerging from the brush, pulling herself along by grasping the fence. She appeared to need it for support.

"Hey, what's wrong," I called as I clambered out of the pit. "Scarlett, what's the trouble?"

"Oh, Tish." Distraught, she pushed back damp ringlets with the back of her wrist. "How far does it go?"

"Does what go?"

Grabbing the fence with both hands, she shook it like an innocent convict. "The fence—where does it go?"

"Cool down, dear. I suppose it goes all around their property. Why so upset?"

Obviously it was a great effort for Scarlett to regain her composure. "I hate fences" seemed like an inadequate explanation for her distress. She might hate fences but clearly there was more to it than that. It was clear too that Scarlett wasn't going to enlarge on the subject. Her attention was diverted by the rock pile.

"Tish, we've got to examine every one of those stones. They may have invaluable ancient markings."

Back in the pit, I was harnessing my illegible rock. "Why don't you leave that up to Walter, Terry and Kay? They want to rebuild the chamber but I don't suppose they'd do it here. That grim fence is a lousy background for a tourist attraction."

The fence didn't make me happy either. Certainly Cootie Razor, Clyde and I weren't going to be able to scale a six-foot fence.

"I wouldn't be surprised if my father felt Sunday's explosion in the rocks of the Burren. He knew there were great temples in New England. To have destroyed one is a cardinal sin. Let's pray to God it's the last one to meet such a fate."

What god, I wondered—the Druid's sun god Bel?

Scarlett helped me carry my rock home.

As we rounded the corner of my house, a huge animal charged at us. I gasped, then recoginzed Cootie Razor. The massive creature saw Lulu and brought her gallop to a halt and with her rump high and her front paws on the ground invited Lulu to play something that looked like patty-cake. They sniffed and goozled, grunted and walked round and round each other. I could see the fleas taking suicidal leaps from Cootie's height onto Lulu's small body.

"Hey, girl, heel, heel."

Clyde's order had to be repeated with increasing emphasis. It finally took effect when I deposited Lulu inside the house. I returned with Lew's red kerchief.

Clyde was examining the rock. "Got some nice stones behind my place. The missus liked them. She was sure the marks on them had been made by Indians. She was an Abenaki."

As we followed Cootie up the hill, I told Clyde to be sure to tell Officer Reed about his rocks. Another time I too would be more interested, but Lew occupied all my thoughts.

Cootie led us to the scattered rocks that had once been the chamber. I hoped her noisy inspection of the site wouldn't attract the Ringers.

"Think she'd like to get to the other side of that fence."

Clyde had heard about the Ringers, his information was that they were nudist, therefore crazy. I agreed, at least with his reasoning. Anyone who would go around naked in Vermont, except possibly for three days in the middle of August, was crazy. I described the cult and told him about the events spurred by my fall.

With sudden enthusiasm Cootie surged uphill. Her long ears slapped against her chops as she moved her head to and fro, parting the ground cover. Breathless, I envied Clyde the advantage of being pulled up the rugged foothills by Cootie's leash. A dozen times I yelled, hey, wait for me. But I assumed they'd notice I was missing when they got wherever they were going. Ten miserable minutes later I came upon them beyond where the fence turned west.

"Guess I'd better stop her, don't you think?" Clyde asked pointing at the dog's angular rump just visible under an umbrella of flying earth and gravel.

Frightened that Cootie was digging her own grave, I helped Clyde tug on her leash. We both sat down hard when she decided to quit. The shock went from my gluteus-maximus to my coccyx, up my spine and nearly broke my ribs all over again.

Cootie collapsed into a mud pie—only her pink tongue revealed which end was on my foot.

"Well, I guess that's where your friend went. Clyde swiped at his halo of mites. Be easier if we were on the other side of the fence."

The damn fence. Using my straw hat and moving gingerly, I filled Cootie's excavation with dirt and leaves. While it needed a little more work to be an ideal escape route, it might give me a good feeling to know there was another way out of Ringer territory in case the front gates were locked.

Resting from the painful effort, I watched Clyde light a kitchen match with his thumb nail. Except for the cigar in his face and a belly that hung over his belt, he was a good looking man. I tried to envision him as a young man married to a willowy Pochahontas.

"Your wife was an Abenaki? From Canada?"

"From Vermont, they're not a lot of them left. She tried not to look like an Indian, or act like an Indian. She wanted to be like a regular American."

"Why, did she make people feel guilty? Did she think she reminded them that the land belonged to the Indians and maybe no one would like her?"

"Something like that". His damp butt began to smoke. "Then she got proud of being an Indian, got interested in Indians, visited her family. She learned they'd been people living in Vermont for more than ten thousand years. Her ancestors."

"Guess they all weren't Indians. Sailors have been landing on America's shores for a couple of thousand years."

"You ask me, I think they should ship some of them back, beginning to get too crowded around here. Come on, you dirty old critter," he prodded Cootie. "We'll follow the fence around, see if she picks up anything else."

A couple of Ringers leaning on shovels watched us pass by the barn. I waved gaily. At the front gate, the dog expressed interest in the ground where Lew and I had stood but it was a path too heavily travelled for her to keep the scent.

If the mission weren't so troublesome, the time spent with the man and dog would have been delightful. Clyde refused my offer of coffee—in a way I was glad. Flea powder was on my mind. A night in bed with Cootie's cooties didn't have any appeal.

After a hot bath and a bout with Ben-Gay, I called Scarlett. I wanted to apologize for my abrupt departure and to assure her that the fence did go all around the cult property, but she wasn't home. Hilary was. He accepted my invitation for dinner and told me he'd bring it—except, of course, for the chocolate roll. I thought it was a well-struck bargain.

With a page of Ogam script from Fell's book on my lap, I tried to decipher the markings on the rock we'd lugged home. There were ten characters, most of which matched the Iberian Ogam alphabet, but they made no sense. I spent an hour twisting and turning the letters with no enlightenment. The only word I was able to spell was 'wee wee' which didn't help me.

I checked my apple green watch. Almost time for Hil.

Hilary had a strong wiry old body but his passion for cashmere made him feel like a kitten. I put his jacket over the back of a kitchen chair and smiled as he unloaded a laundry basket of food and equipment. A steamer for the beautiful long-stemmed brussel sprouts. The ill-fitting top of my vegetable steamer didn't come up to his standards. There were seedless grapes to be added to the sprouts before serving. Lulu retrieved a nutmeg that rolled across the floor. Hilary used nutmeg the way the Chinese used monosodium glutamate, to enhance everything. He removed two cans of salmon.

"Canned salmon?"

"We're having a souffle."

"Oh, Lord, Hilary, that's an hour an and half away. I poured our drinks. I'll be tight as a coot." Which reminded me of the day's adventures which I recounted.

The contents of a double boiler were exhibited for my inspection. Of course, my thoughtful chef had prepared the cream sauce base for the souffle in advance.

"Only an hour to booze it up." He straddled a

chair. "Some state archeologist came this morning. You didn't seem to be anyplace around so I took him up the hill. He was a nice enough little gent but he couldn't seem to work up much enthusiasm for the idea of visiting Celts.

"He said the state acknowledges pre-Colombian excursions into the state and he pointed out that Indians were not known to have done any stone work, preferring wood and hide. They also usually settled by the rivers. The fact that most rock chambers were located on uplands and hilltops and not in the valleys made them interesting. He said that while there is no evidence of pre-Colombian European settlement in the state, that doesn't mean that evidence of such settlements might not be identified in the future. He wasn't a total wet blanket, but he made it clear that the current belief is that these chambers are examples of rural nineteenth century Vermont. He deplored, with me, their lack of protection and preservation. He thinks the zest for a new interpretation of our past may really stir up some serious investigations that might even change the mind of academe. Tried to keep him here for you but he had to get back to Montpelier."

Hilary passed me our favorite hors d'oeuvre—thin pita bread brushed with butter, dusted with Parmesan and then baked. They were so crisp and light I kidded myself they weren't fattening.

"How did this fellow explain the Ogam script?"

"Scars, marks from tools, but I think he's wrong. It's almost time that the tables got turned. Maybe the complacent set should explain to the new explorers just what was going on for the two or three thousand years before Colombus. After all, they do concede the Vikings were here even though they left little evidence and very few runes."

Runes, Hilary explained, was the alphabet used by ancient Germanic and Scandavian people. Runic markings were to be found all along the coast of New England.

Hilary provides generously which is fortunate because Walter arrived and, after having a drink, was easily persuaded to stay for dinner.

We reported on events and the conversation with the archeologist.

"Have you ever checked your property for stone work, Hilary? Maybe," Walter added, "it's too high, but the orientation for the summer solstice would be right on that shoulder of the hill." Hilary shook his head. Walter went on, "Through the years before I came to the ski area, there's no telling how many rock sites were probably knocked over for trails. But maybe we should go look. You know how much we want that land, Hilary. What good does it do you? Why don't you change your mind?"

"Don't answer that, Hil," I said. "It's sickening to watch our mountains being seduced by sports kooks and developers." A couple of drinks brought me up to boiling point. "In most cases, whole mountains are raped. These creeps came to our mountains because they were so beautiful and now they're ruining them."

"Oh, come on, Tish," Walter said. "Skiing is exciting and it doesn't hurt the hills. The lifts and rides make lots of people happy."

"And you rich."

"And the condos and chalets," he said. "You know that trees can grow six feet in a year. Places being built now you won't even see in six years."

"I happen to think it's the beginning of the end of the Vermont landscape—but let's not talk about it any more. I don't want to ruin Hil's dinner."

We had an after-dinner drink in the studio. Tomorrow was the day I planned to paint The Marshall. He had returned a day earlier than expected. An underling had called and informed me that his boss was troubled by chills and draughts and would sit for his portrait in his office. In spite of having to cope with changing light and having to tote my gear, I was pleased that my entry to Amber Trees was to be so simple.

"Kay tells me the thing he wears around his neck is a gold prique, at least I think that's how you say it when it's jewelry."

Walter frowned. "No kidding, Tish. You watch out for Alan Smith, Marshall, or whatever his name is. Don't mistake him for some kind of pussy cat. Watch it."

"Watch it. I'll be watching him. Not only are portrait painters people watchers. Unwittingly they record qualities that some might not observe. The same way I can, against my will, record a vacant look in my model's eyes, I can, still unconsciously, record evil or anger. Often I don't realize what I've revealed in a face until I see the portrait months or years later."

Hilary began to pack his basket. "By God, that souffle was good."

It was a relief to hear him say it. I knew it was good and Walter knew it was good but if Hilary had the slightest doubt about the excellence of one of his epicurean creations, the analysis could last for half an hour, longer than I expected to stay awake.

10

Thank goodness I managed to arrange my usually mobile face into a dead pan. I had to supress almost uncontrollable laughter when I was ushered into the Marshal's office.

Seated in an oversize arm chair (or was it a throne?) the head of the Ring of Right was huddled under a blanket that had been removed from a Hilton Hotel. His feet were submerged in a plastic wash tub. Steam rose up his bare legs showing that pattern of hair displayed by long-time garter wearers. His right hand held a round plastic inhaler to his chest. It filled the room with the smell of eucalyptus. Obviously, the chief hadn't heard me over the hiss of the machine. His head pinned a telephone to his shoulder. The Wall Street Journal, in what little lap his fat stomach left, was folded subway size.

"For Christ sake, get on it, Harry. We could lose three points while you're arranging your ass in the chair."

He turned when the female Ringer who had escorted me to his office touched his arm.

"Call me at closing", he snarled at poor Harry. His handmaiden unplugged the inhaler and removed it. He looked unhappy parting with the newspaper. She took the telephone and sprayed the receiver with an aerosol can and wiped it with a tissue. Was he afraid of catching his own germs?

"Can you paint me with this on, Ma'am?" His query, like his voice, now was docile. I detected a slight accent, maybe a little bit of Brit left over from a Liverpool infancy?

"I guess it's possible. Do you want Hilton Hotel painted right side up or the way it is?"

His pudgy face hardened. Maybe I should give regard to Walter's suggestion to watch out. The guru might be a little short on humor with his feet soaking and his stocks sinking.

I explained that we would have to decide on just what costume to choose for the portrait. Especially if the painting was to include hand and arms—legs and knees. (Lord how I hated to paint knees). Most clients relished the choosing process. My usual instructions were that a model should wear something becoming—a good shape, a flattering collar or neck line and that whatever garment was chosen should be classic and timeless. Unless you were Tina Turner and of course wanted to look NOW.

Reluctantly The Marshal turned back a corner of his blanket and gave me a peek of the red fabric underneath.

"Pretty red. Sort of papal, isn't it? How far down does it go?" I felt like some old roue asking a maiden to undress.

Finally, unveiled, he handed his blanket to the girl. The tent-like tunic stopped at his bare knees. A chain-link gold colored belt lent a Renaissance touch. The golden phallus hung on a chain around his neck. Another chain held a magnifying glass. His jerkin had a Nehru collar which minimized his porky neck. A mousey hair piece didn't help his bland features.

Often men were easier to paint than women because a pronounced feature like heavy eyebrows or a big nose or a cleft chin was something to hang on to—if you got the eyebrows right it looked like the model.

But Alan Smith's face was as hopeless as his name. Thick putty-colored skin didn't help either. A sculptor would have considered him unfinished. No good bones, no dents or bumps.

I'd coped with worse and I knew that soon he'd begin to show me what he thought was important about his face. That would help.

Many sitters feel they have a good and bad side. He was no different. He was arranging himself in profile, one hand hooked in his belt, the other grasping the chair arm. The dimples below the summit of his knuckles revolted me.

While I wrestled my folding easel into a geometric stance, he asked me how long it would take to paint the portrait.

"Depends on how large it is and if I get a good start," I smiled, I hope winningly, "and if you're a good model."

"What is good?"

"Someone who holds the pose in a relaxed manner. When we decide on the pose, I can rig up a mirror so you can watch me paint."

I can see he thought that was a boring suggestion. Maybe the handmaiden should stand in front of him and turn the pages of Money magazine.

"Just as long as you do it fast" was his ungracious comment. With soft charcoal I started drawing on a 24 x 30-inch sheet of paper. Even his fat knees wouldn't bother me if it would give me time to look around for Lew. If I started a big painting, I could keep the body sketchy so I didn't have to finish it if I had any luck with my search. My sitter was nodding which gave me an idea of how I could use Kay to keep him somnolent.

Bold strokes on the paper outlined his leaden figure, I used the side of the charcoal to make dark areas. With red conte crayon I worked on his hands. They struck me as greedy and coarse. For the first time I noticed a wide metal band on his ring finger. The Ring of Right?

When he jerked awake, I asked him about the band. He brought the ring up to his nose as though he'd never seen it before and said "no".

"What shall I call you? Mr. Smith?"

He shrugged his larded shoulders.

"If you want to."

"What does the Ring of Right stand for, Mr. Smith? Nobody seems to know."

"Right."

"You mean right as opposed to left or right as opposed to wrong?"

"That's right."

"What do you all do?" I tried to sound like a TV hostess. "Work in the greenhouses? What do you grow? I do like to know more about the people I paint. Or perhaps you'd rather I didn't ask any questions?"

"We grow food." He adjusted his collar. "My head aches."

"Oh, I'm sorry." Then I took a chance and asked the hulk if he knew a young man called Lew Weber. I got another thudding negative.

How could a totally uncharismatic character like

The Marshal inspire the devotion or even the attention of his disciples? His crisp commands to Harry the broker had been his only sign of vitality.

Painting him would be impossible if I gave in to my inclination to loathe the man. I'd have to keep trying to understand him or the portrait would be appalling.

Before I left, I took a roll of black and white Polaroid pictures of my model. If he slept as much as I wanted him to I wouldn't be seeing much of his face.

The Marshal expressed no interest in seeing what I had accomplished in an hour of work. He declared the session was over and to be continued the next morning at the same time.

My escort was waiting outside the door. She walked with me to the gate. Consulting her watch she said she would meet me at ten tomorrow morning.

No good bye—not even "Have a nice day". Not the slightest smile nor any friendly gesture. She'd be a problem if she hung around while I painted.

Kay was tickled at the prospect of reading to my sitter. We discussed at length the soporific qualities of available books. She favored a history of Vermont but I felt Ethan Allen might excite Smith. "The History of the Dutch Reform Church in America" was one of our choices. I suggested "Two Years Before the Mast" or even better "The Ancient Mariner" rendered in sing-song pentameter.

If I gave a damn about my sitter there would be a lot of absorbing decisions to make. In any event, I did have to decide on the size of the painting and stretch a canvas, which I accomplished in the serene light of my studio.

To understand the joy of north light, gather some objects, a pitcher, fruit, a book and put them on a table under a high north window and you'll see why the light is beloved by artists. Shadows stay the same whether the day is bright or dark. Forms, foreheads, apples, bottles or whatever—all seem bound together in painterly harmony.

The changing light from the windows in The Marshal's office was disconcerting. There were times when painting a portrait taught you something, times when you could really study the model. This was not such an occasion. A flair for achieving a likeness and an old professional's know-how would, I hope, let me paint a good portrait of him with no real concentration.

After stretching the canvas, I transfered the drawing I had done using a sheet of yellow carbon paper. Proceeding in this fashion, I wouldn't have to worry about the drawing while I painted. Painting a child I would have started to paint with no drawing, to catch the color and spontaneity. Another method would be the ancient technique of underpainting with egg tempura. You shake up an egg with equal parts oil and water (oil and water do mix) and then with a brush and dry powdered white you build up a bas-relief of the model. Color is added with oil and pigment glazes, more tempura, more oil, fat on lean until the end when you add the darkest accents. The tough part of this procedure is that you can't change your mind once you've started. If you choose to move a nostril half an inch to the right, or tilt an eyebrow in a different direction, the underpainting will glow through, getting more luminous with age. This quality accounts for the wonderous glowing flesh of the old masters.

But I didn't want to spend any more time recording The Marshal's unlovely flesh than was absolutely necessary.

Walter called to inquire about my meeting with The Marshal.

"Hope you don't mind, Tish, but I took the liberty of studying the stone on your front porch. I realize the inscription isn't old. I figure there must be some reason for it."

Using Fell's section on alphabets he said he had come to the conclusion that it said "my mink". Of course, in both cases, Walter and I had ignored a few unmanageable letters. "My mink" or "wee wee", somehow I felt our interpretations weren't going to add a new dimension to the understanding of archeology.

Dinner was relaxing, especially because I knew Hilary had an engagement and wasn't likely to come barging in and catch me eating frozen diet manicotti. Reading the names of the chemicals listed on the package was bad for his blood pressure.

Before I turned out my light that night I studied the scratches and scrawls that represented my attempt to decipher the Ogam inscription, with the hope that the brain I couldn't command when asleep could do a better job of translating than the daytime brain I was supposed to be in charge of.

Sometimes it works. I nearly knocked Lulu off the bed when I sat bolt upright at three a.m. The inscription wasn't written in Ogam. I wasn't written in Iberian, Punic or Runic. It was written in plain old English. I turned on the light and examined the original letters. Some were tilted and the 'K' was on its back, but it clearly spelt two words—Phoebe's Knee.

Lulu cocks her head when asked a direct question.

"What in hell does Phoebe's Knee mean?"

Phoebe Alexander, Phoebe Knowles, Phoebe Gill, maybe I could think of other friends named Phoebe but what about their knees? It was crazy. At three-thirty I took a couple of aspirin, my version of sleeping pills. As usual, they worked.

11

I don't know how Kay managed to look so demure. Her gorgeous hair was pulled back in a pony tail. Her white painter's overalls were immaculate and she carried a Mickey Mouse school bag full of books.

My canvas was propped up against the open doorway of Amber Trees. I rested my paint box and a can of turpentine on the porch. No one had stopped us at the gate and I thought it would be wise if we waited a few minutes to see if The Marshal's handmaiden would appear.

Kay's nose twitched like a bunny's. "Smell it?"

My olfactory equipment isn't the best.

"Smell what?"

"Pot, heavy pot."

"At this hour of the morning?" I said primly. My Swatch said ten o'clock. "Sort of an early beginning for a Saturday night rumble."

While we waited, I told Kay about Pheobe's Knee and asked her to bring the name up in conversation to see if my model had any reaction.

Our escort appeared and looked at her watch. Glad I was wearing my tri-focals so I could see it too. An electronic black model with time digits at the top of the face, below, flashing on and off in red letters, were the words 'OH GOD'. Did OH GOD mean oh God damn or oh lord God?

We followed her upstairs. I nudged Kay.

"She's going to be a pain in the neck."

Kay knew that I intended to inspect the house while my subject was asleep. She insisted that she too would make exploratory forays if the opportunity presented itself.

The Marshal looked at Kay and turned to me with the closest thing to an expression I'd ever seen on his face. A questioning look.

When I introduced them, Kay moved forward with her hand outstretched. He pulled back causing ripples in his foot bath and raised both palms warding off contact.

Kay gave him a dazzling smile. "I'm not afraid of germs, Mr. Smith."

"I am. Stand back. Why," he asked me, "why do we need this lady?"

Kay took over, displaying the books and explained her mission. She pulled up a straight chair and sat in front of him, a cautious few yards away.

He rejected our stunning literary choices and pressed a button on the intercom. He raised the receiver. "Bring in the paper." It was an order, not a request. The telephone seemed to plug into a vein of authority in his sluggish system. He snatched a copy of Barron's from a fleet-footed Ringer without a word of thanks. He shoved the paper at Kay.

"What would you like me to read?" Kay asked.

I could tell from the lilt of her voice that she was still trying to charm the man. She'd find out soon enough it wasn't possible. I did laugh out loud when he asked her to start off by reading the high and low quotations of the most active stocks of the week.

It was the first time I'd ever painted a portrait

against a background of stock quotations. It was quite relaxing.

Not only did I prefer my own north light, but subjects posing in their homes were in charge of events and vulnerable to interruptions. In my studio they seemed to leave a little ego and a lot of troubles outside the door.

The relationship between sitter and artist was usually a happy one and often quite revealing, perhaps on both sides of the easel. Sitters seem to want you to know more about them than the physical facade. Sometimes it was the beginning of a friendship.

With a small oval palette hooked on my thumb, I squeezed out blobs of paint—white, black and yellow ochre, enough color for the first day. With wide brushes, wet with turpentine, I worked quickly. Kay, pointing at my sleeping model, said "Old Fatso's in snoozy-bye land." She continued to read quotations in a soothing voice. "IBM down from a high of 150 points to minus zero."

"Tell him I've gone to the john."

I darted out of the room. No handmaiden. The halls were empty. I started towards the back of the house. I wasn't so naive that I expected Lew to pop out of a room and say oh, gee whizz, how glad he was to see me, but I did expect to get a good idea of the layout. Maybe I could eliminate some areas from a future search.

I looked through open doors along the back hall. They were used as dormitories. They were obviously cared for by indifferent and careless tenants. Towards the front of the house were two bedrooms with a large bathroom in between. They both had four-poster beds, massive armoires and chiffoniers. In one I admired a fine Eastlake cheval glass and in the other room an object I coveted, an S shape Victorian conversation chair. It would make a great prop for a double portrait.

Inside the bathroom, I closed the doors. No enema bags dangling from hooks. So much for that rumor. The grubby medicine cabinet held nothing of interest. What did I expect? But dozens of pills and potions arranged on a separate shelf attested to The Marshal's concern for his health.

The wide porch roof directly under the double hung window was reassuring, though I hoped I'd never have to make an exit that way. Jumping off roofs was an activity I'd given up a half century ago.

Kay was softly singing three blind mice when I returned.

"I think the old hypochondriac is stirring"

He assumed his pose without comment.

Kay's voice rose. "Tell me, Tish. Have you been feeling Phoebe's knee lately?" Then, even louder, "How is Pheobe's knee feeling?"

The Marshal frowned. "Phoebe's what?"

"Knee," Kay said. "Have you seen Phoebe's knee?"

He shook his head and pushed the intercom button. I couldn't hear what he said but in a few minutes a Ringer came in with a steaming tea kettle and added its contents to the foot bath. He gestured for Kay to continue.

When he began snoring, I pointed up and ran out on tiptoe and up the carpeted stairs to the third floor. The smell of pot intensified. I turned right and peeked in a half-open door. I hoped the pair on the bed hadn't heard my gasp of surprise. A man was in a frenzy of activity, his bare rump bouncing in the air.

I had no wish to watch their sexual acrobatics and even less wish to be caught doing so.

I almost ran into the next room which, thank heavens, was empty. The repugnant poster over the bed was one I had seen, a nude model intertwined with a boa constrictor. What kept me in the room was the view from the window. Even on the third floor, the windows were tall with graceful lines. I liked the generous sills and heavy sash. The view featured the parking lot.

There was a robin's-egg blue sedan, but no faded blue Volvo. But, to identify the make of a car from that height was impossible. Probably they'd painted the car, a matter of an hour's work. Certainly the Ringers wouldn't be foolish enough to leave Lew's car in plain sight, painted or unpainted.

Back in the hall I looked around for a door to the attic. Was there an attic? I scolded myself for not examining the house carefully from the outside.

In the front hall I came upon a relaxed Ringer. He was balancing on the back legs of a dainty French chair, his head resting against a closed door. The weed between his lips was smoking.

Barely opening his eyes, he wiggled the fingers of one hand at me.

"Hi ho everybody, how's tricks?"

"Hi ho," I replied companionably, wiggling my fingers in return. "I've come to see Phoebe. Is she in her room?" I advanced firmly, "I want to see her knee."

His eyebrows rose in mild exasperation, I guess at having to deal with an elderly kook.

"Phoebe, shmeebe. I don't give a flying fuck about Phoebe. Go away, lady. You better ... "

I don't know what he was going to say next because at that point all hell broke loose.

Kay was yelling, The Marshal was roaring and feet pounded on the stairways. The guard jumped to his feet, the chair became kindling beneath him. He ran down the hall. I dashed for the stairs, colliding with the lovers. I had time to muse in flight that togas were ideal for emergency dressing.

"Call a doctor." I knew that was Kay's voice.

For a second I couldn't decide whether to run out of the house and find a doctor or to go see what had happened. The door to Smith's office was jammed with Ringers. Inspired, I ran back upstairs to the door that had been guarded by old smokey. It was locked. I banged on the panels. Nothing happened. No response. No sound.

Once again running downstairs, I caught a glimpse of a woman running down the front stairway. I recognized Scarlett's red hair. Calling her was useless. The place was in a turmoil.

This time I insisted on being admitted to The Marshal's office. He was stretched out on the floor. The Ringer crouched over him was administering mouth to mouth artificial respiration. He stopped as I watched. He nodded with satisfaction and waved the group away. He beckoned to a hefty Ringer who picked up the boss and between them they led the mumbling guru to one of the front bedrooms. The disciples followed.

In a moment we were alone. Kay put her head in her hands. "What a madhouse, what a fucking madhouse."

"What happened?"

"Someone tried to kill him."

I sat on the window sill with my arms folded waiting for Kay to get a grip on herself.

"He was snoring, Tish, so I went out that door," she pointed, "just to see where it went. It's just a little room with a typewriter, computer equipment, file cabinets and stuff. Maybe I was in there three minutes. I had this funny feeling I better get back and you wouldn't believe it but your model was all hunched over with one hand in the foot bath, the other clutching his wig, and he was making this awful noise, like a frog saying ahhh.

"Then I saw the hair dryer in the water. Funny how you see everything so clearly. I could see it was plugged in and it dawned on me he'd been electrocuted. I didn't dare touch him. I flicked the only switch I could see then I yelled my head off."

"You poor kid, how awful."

"First that girl came. She was numb, just looked at him. Then everyone came. What a racket! They got him on the floor. I was the first to find the phone and I dialed the rescue squad when someone grabbed the phone out of my hand and said forget it, or words to that effect. I tried to insist, I suggested the police. The guy told me in an ugly way to mind my own business and suggested I keep my mouth shut and get the hell out. Who'd want to kill him?"

"Dozens of people probably stood in line just waiting for the chance," I said.

"It's no joke, Tish. Do you think someone tried to kill him for his money? Where does he get all that money for the stock market?"

"Robbing banks?"

"Maybe. I bet they grow marijuana in those greenhouses."

"They haven't had time to grow a crop, much less harvest one."

"I wish you'd tell me, why does Scarlett think they're so great?"

Scarlett. I'd almost forgotten her. "Kay, what did Scarlett do? Was she any help?"

"Scarlett? I didn't see anyone but Ringers."

I wondered out loud if the electrocution could have been an accident, but we discounted the possibility, crediting Smith with more sense than to be waving an electric instrument over a trough of water. She described the dryer as small but powerful.

"Probably the current isn't strong enough to burn you, like in the electric chair, but I think that amount of current could stop your heart. Especially if you were a super-hypochondriac."

"I'm tempted," she added, "to call Charlie Reed."

I was against that idea. The thought that my obsession with Lew had put Kay in any kind of danger made me sick.

Kay did her bunny sniff again.

"A little thing like attempted murder isn't going to stop those jerks from getting thoroughly stoned tonight."

"Ah, the Saturday night mentality. Let's get out of here before we get potted just inhaling their old smoke."

12

Charlie Reed's squad car was parked outside my house. He was sitting on the front porch looking at my rock. He had just returned from a meeting of the Early Sites Research Society and was bursting with enthusiasm.

Even if I had thought it was wise to tell him about the electrocution episode, I couldn't have slipped a word in edgewise.

"Phoebe's Knee," I said. I repeated Phoebe's Knee a couple of times until he finally stopped talking. Then I explained my esoteric translation of the message on the rock.

He studied the markings again and wrote the letters in his notebook. He conceded that it did spell Phoebe's Knee.

"But what does it mean?"

I recited the surnames of the Phoebes I knew and then with sudden illumination I remembered another Phoebe.

"Lew Weber's grandmother's pug was called Phoebe."

He was not transported by my information.

"And her knee, did your friend Lew discuss his grandmother's dog's knee?"

Sarcasm wasn't becoming to Charlie, but he did have the courtesy to discuss the matter for a while, but neither of us could come up with any explanation for the cryptic words on the rock.

Launching into his favorite topic, Charlie talked about the meeting and described with excitement the archeological findings near the end of the Thames River in Connecticut. He told me about the stone architectural ruins there on the coast. The script carved on the ledges pointed to a clear connection with Christian Celts during the late Iron Age. Other worn Ogam inscriptions in the area were found to be similar to ones in Ireland and Scotland. He described the hundreds of Roman coins that had been found in the Thames basin. How much more proof, Charlie wanted to know, did a body need to believe that the Indians had lots of company.

Hilary joined us, producing a large white carton. Hot fish chowder from Manchester's elegant super market.

Charlie's departure was a relief. I couldn't put my mind on archeology. Hilary and I ate our soup in the late summer sunshine.

"How about dinner at the Inn tonight, Tish?"

I claimed painful ribs to decline, but truthfully I'd forgotten about my ribs. I had other plans for the evening. Hilary's reaction to the rock's message wasn't as polite as Charlie's. He advised me to soft pedal the news.

"Talking about somebody's dog's knee might make the local gentry think you're whacko. I don't think it will help your cause of finding the boy, talking about a grandmother who had a dog, who had a knee."

I shut up because I knew he was right, though he did admit that the letters spelled Phoebe's knee.

Hilary let Lulu lick his soup plate. "Something's going on in town and I don't like it." He had my attention. "I talked to trooper Charlie in the store before he came over here. He doesn't want to alarm anyone but some heavies are moving into Lofton."

"Heavies, you mean Ringers?"

"Heavies is his word. Charlie doesn't know. His instructions are to be alert. He plans to stick around town more and he wants me to keep an eye out for any action." He anticipated my question. "Any action, anything even slightly unusual."

Like trying to kill my model, I wondered? Kay had promised me, against her will, not to tell anyone about the electrocution until after the weekend. Even if the law investigated a report from Kay, I knew everything would be denied by the Ringers. We'd look like fools and I'd have lost some ground in my search for Lew.

Certainly my veracity as a witness, given my bias, would be questioned. Maybe I would tell Charlie about it myself, tomorrow. Maybe.

After Hilary left, curiosity led me down the street to Scarlett's house. Her station wagon was in the garage. I opened the front door a crack and yelled "Yoo hoo".

Terry Fink came out of the living room. "Come on in. Scarlett's on the phone."

Terry's designer denims made the corn cob pipe he was smoking seem the last word in sophistication. Tired eyes robbed him of his usual boyish look. I preferred the solemn man to the charming boniface.

"Tish, what are we going to do with these stinking Ringers? They're going to ruin our business. How would you like to come to the Inn for a bucolic weekend full of quaint charm and find those grim hippies next door? I wouldn't. Marty could dish up escargots, fiddlehead ferns and every kind of croissant known to man and it still wouldn't bring guests back if they thought they'd have to look at the leaves turn with those stringy-haired bimbos standing on their heads all over the place."

Scarlett blew me a kiss and sat down on the couch while Terry was talking.

"It's a bitter pill," she said, "but I have to admit the Ringers are not behaving the way I expected them to. I just wish I knew what to do about it."

"What were you doing with them yesterday when I saw you in the house?"

Scarlett looked surprised. She said I must be mistaken. What a liar! I hoped my reaction wasn't too obvious. I took a deep breath and decided to make an amusing story about painting the portrait and life with The Marshal in general. I skipped the electrical episode.

"I'd like to murder the guy. But," Terry added, "of course I'd make it look like an accident."

Scarlett looked down at her hands, turning them over a couple of time, as though she was deciding whether to keep them. She then used them to momentarily cover her eyes.

"I'll think of something. After all, it's my fault they're here."

"Not entirely. After all, we on the zoning board okayed the whole deal," I said. "It's not just your fault."

"But I knew Alan Smith before he came to Lofton."

Terry and I were both surprised.

She told us she had met Alan Smith in Wilkes Barre a year earlier and he had told her about his group, which he described as students of life. They practised simplicity, he said, and learned to cope with life as it was. A quiet group, he assured her. Farm land was important because contact with the soil was a basic act of realism that would help them in their search for Right.

"What do they mean by Right?" Terry asked.

She shrugged. "I guess I didn't ask. At the time we met, Smith wore regular clothes, a business suit. He looked completely acceptable. Guess I'm gullible. As you know, there were those two farms on the market and I reasoned that it would be better for Lofton to have single ownership rather than having the land chopped up into lots or ringed with condominiums."

Scarlett seemed flustered when I asked her if she had found out exactly why the Ringers had blown up the rock chamber. The same reason, she said, that we had been been given. That Smith didn't know about it.

"Smith must have known about the dynamite. It's not something you buy casually."

Terry stood up. "Wonder what else they plan to blow up. Some time soon I'm going to sneak down and take a good look at the farms. If those jerks are really farming, I'll be a guru."

Scarlett told us that tomorrow in church she planned to plead with the congregation to return the Druid rocks. She thought, aided by her father's books, the temple could probably be reconstructed.

If we could read each others' minds I guess there'd be no such thing as civilization. Certainly polite society wouldn't exist. No one read my mind. No one even said a word about Lew Weber. Did they think that my meeting with him was an aberration? I guessed that Terry was thinking about business. Was Scarlett thinking about the Celtic temple or her lie?

She held my arm when Terry left.

"When will you finish the portrait?"

"I could finish it tomorrow or three weeks from now."

"Tomorrow, Tish, please. I'm nervous about the Ringers. I have a nasty old-country premonition that something evil could happen at Amber Trees. My father filled me full of Druid lore and a particularly unhappy omen is to see a bat fly up your chimney. Last night a bat flew down my chimney and before I could think what to do, he flew back up. Silly, I know, but please be speedy with the portrait. Better yet, tell Smith it's done and don't go back at all."

She had a point. Why didn't I call my travel agent in Manchester and tell her to book me on the next flight to Athens? I'd like to sink into a classic mood, eat stewed lamb, drink retsina and paint some Mediterranean landscapes. A small chat with the Oracle at Delphi might help, but she'd probably say the same thing, "Forget about what's-his-name".

Dispirited, I walked home reviewing my plans for the evening. Lulu pranced around in anticipation when I got out her leash. I wasn't going to take a chance of having her give me away to the Ringers while I worked on the trough that Cootie Razor had begun under the fence.

Trying to dig under the far side of the fence was agony. The handle of my hoe was too long and my trowel was too small. Only the image of myself stuck halfway through my escape route kept me going.

Resting on my haunches, I realized the excavation was more than a way to escape. It would serve too as a splendid entrance to Ringer territory.

The Ringers didn't seem to feel it was necessary to patrol the fence. And, for that matter, I couldn't understand why anyone would want to get inside except for a special reason, like mine. Don't think, I warned myself. You have work to do.

Lord knows when the Ringers ate dinner or even if they ate, but nine o'clock seemed like a good time to start my search.

My costume took time. A toga-type robe is deceivingly simple. I found that a slit cut for my head in the middle of the length of monks cloth, wasn't enough. I felt I'd be more mobile with sleeves, making them was tricky. My gray exercise pants would be perfect. Not only would they stay in place if I decided to stand on my head, but they had two zip pockets. Comfortable old ballet slippers seemed ideal for tiptoeing.

My wig on second inspection looked too light in color and texture. Rummaging around I found what I wanted—a comb I had bought years ago to minimize my gray hair. It came in a case lined with a brown waxy substance. With many combings, the wig took on a mousy overtone and made the hair look as stringy as The Marshal's handmaidens'.

With my small round glasses and no makeup I felt sure I'd pass as one of the disciples.

Over a bourbon and a peanut butter sandwich I tried to think carefully about my preparations. First on the list was a rechargeable flashlight smaller than a clip of matches. Next, a plastic charge card. Once upon a time Hilary had tried to show me how to open a simple lock using a card. I'm a poor pupil and wasn't a bit interested at the time, but I figured that in a pinch I could make it work. I was thinking of that room on the third floor.

The last item was a real inspiration. I'd been wondering how to protect myself if one of the heftier goons chose to maul me. My travel-size can of hair spray was the answer. About the size of a magic marker, it would be an effective weapon.

God bless the National Geographic shows on television. One kept me from going mad waiting for my watch to say nine. A handsome young man and his beautiful wife had spent three years recording the mating habits of the tree sloth. After an hour of dangerous-looking sex and a successful birthing, I flicked off the tube and prepared to leave.

When I hugged Lulu, I noticed my Swiss army knife and put it in my pocket. A wizard tool, just feeling it there gave me confidence.

I left by the back door. It would be embarassing to be stopped by a Loftonite—my masquerade wasn't intended to fool friends. I skittered along just beyond the edge of the street. A couple of times I hid from car lights. My heart was pounding when I finally stood in the shadow of Amber Trees' stone gate posts.

Possibly the couple kissing a few yards off on my right were supposed to be quarding the gate. I didn't dare walk by them. My trip might be ended before it began if one of them saw me. I decided to stand very still and hope the love-making would progress to a degree of total absorption, or, with luck, they might feel that their activities required more privacy and move out of sight.

While I waited, I observed the house. Lighted windows were scattered all over the facade. Shades or curtains on the first floor prevented me from seeing any action. The topmost light came from a room on the third floor. I looked through the trees at the third floor windows. If there were an attic above, it was not evident on the exterior of the house.

The necking couple had finally disappeared behind

a dense juniper. I quickly walked through the gate and then through the larger opening of the chain link fence, I moved sideways facing the house. When my blood pressure returned to normal, I strolled across the yard towards the back of the house. I wanted to see exactly where the other doors of Amber Trees were located.

"Pssst . . . hey Gerta."

I crouched into a ball in the moonless night hoping to resemble a bush.

The voice insisted. "Come on over. We have some great stuff. Hurry up, El Pricko is patrolling the grounds."

I didn't like the sound of El Pricko, but I certainly couldn't get cozy and share pot or sniff coke with the inmates. Someone was walking towards me. With as much serenity as I could muster I cradled my head in my folded hands, and with the weight shared by my forearms, slowly rose into the head stand. I tried to imagine my old instructor telling me to close my eyes and breath deeply. The folds of my robe hid my face. I heard a woman's voice, her robe brushed against mine.

"Leave her alone. You know how she is."

Her companion grunted and their low voices receded. Thank God I was well-balanced and concentrating on my posture or El Pricko's hands on either side of my calves would have sent me tumbling in fright. His breath on my ankles felt damp. It must be emphysema or a hairy nose that made him sound so horrible. His hands moved down my legs to my thighs. Gutteral words that sounded like 'yum, yum' convinced me that El Pricko was not going to make a docile retreat. Enunciating as clearly as possible and with what I hope was cool indifference I said "Get your fucking hands off me."

A little intake of breath suggested his surprise, the pressure of his hands lessened, but he didn't move.

I tried again. "The Marshal is watching us."

That did it. He let go of me instantly. I could hear him jogging away.

Crumpled in my bush pose, I quivered like jelly. I felt my thighs, expecting to feel some hideous primal goo left by his hot hands. At least I'd learned something. The Marshal really was the boss. For a fleeting moment he engendered a surge of warmth.

I crawled under the prickly branches of a balsam tree and considered my next move.

13

Crouched like a Moslem I watched two men and a woman emerge from the shadows near the fence. They walked within a foot of me and went up the porch steps. On my feet again, I was in time to see the Ringers' robes flowing through the door. It closed behind them with a well-oiled thud.

Given the cult's propensity for fake beards and wigs, how could I be sure of the gender of the robed creatures that had passed by me? The way to tell a man from a woman, I'd been advised by a friend, was to unzip them, a maneuver that seemed inappropriate at the moment.

Pressed against the wall, I made my way to the back door. It was open and I could hear voices and the occasional clink of glasses and the duller sounds made by crockery. The long square of light on the grass made me skirt around the area. The rumor about electric lights was another canard. I hid in a bruising tangle of evergreens. My fingers were sticky with resin and I worried about losing my wig.

An unexpected surprise waited for me on the west side of the building, a fire escape. Hidden by tall trees, it had never been visible to me before. It went from the third floor down to the ground. I should have expected it. Amber Trees, once a nursing home, would have been required to have a fire escape.

The iron stairway looked solid; the railings looked substantial. The treads were a single piece of metal and the risers were shallow. What more, I mused, could an old house-breaker ask for.

I scurried up the first flight like a squirrel and paused on the landing level with the second floor. The second floor height was equivalent to three stories in a conventional building. My giddy reaction to heights made me feel squeamish about tackling the next flight.

Experts would have it that many phobias, especially acrophobia, are pure indulgence. Many of us disagree. For me, the physical signal of my distress is my knees which are suddenly robbed of an essential glue that holds them together. That, along with an almost uncontrollable urge to plunge to my doom make me a lousy companion on the edge of a precipice.

Thoughts of the locked room on the third floor stiffened my determination. I tried to will some starch into my legs. A few minutes of yoga breathing kept my heart from audible beating. My mind control wasn't quite as successful. Would a viewer see the resemblance in my ascent to that of Joan of Arc climbing her pyre, or did I look like Miss Marple on Halloween?

Clutching the railings, and counting the steps to distract my mind, I rose, I hoped unseen, to the third floor platform. The trick was to open the window before I succumbed to my suicidal urges.

As I held my breath and pulled, the sash moved up without a sound. I thanked the Victorians and I thanked the skill of Vermont carpenters. I closed the window behind me and, giddy with relief, counted the blessing that the hall ceiling light was not lighted and that the comforting gloom was accompanied by silence.

The next hallway was brighter but still no sounds, no murmurs, no creaking boards. Kneeling in front of the door that had been guarded this morning, I produced my credit card and inserted it between the door and the molding. Gently I turned the knob and used a little pressure. It wasn't locked!

I put away my card and got out my flashlight. It took an eternity to push the door all the way open. I expect criminals to hide behind doors, and I was relieved when the knob finally bumped the plaster wall. Light from the hall illuminated the tiny room. We used to call a room this size on the third floor a maid's room. A cot by the window was covered with an army blanket, a hook on the wall held empty wire coat hangers. An oval mirror hung over a pine chest of drawers but there was nothing to indicate who the occupant had been.

Disappointed, I opened the closet door and felt my first glimmer of hope. Aside from a couple of Ringer costumes and a soiled terry cloth bathrobe, were a pair of the most disreputable sneakers I'd seen since that day that seemed a million years ago when I met Lew Weber. Possibly there were seventeen million sneakers that looked like these in the United States and certainly at least three hundred thousand in Vermont, but for some insane reason these looked familiar.

Thinking about the sneakers, I forgot about my vulnerable role of intruder. There were no sounds from the hall. As I closed the closet door and turned to leave, I gasped at the silhouette that filled the open doorway. The hulking figure stepped forward and pushed the door closed behind him.

"Now," he said, "The Marshal isn't watching."

My instincts for survival are extremely acute, thanks to a childhood spent trying to escape the tortures devised by two maniacal boys who lived next door to us in Wellesley. When I realized my would-be roommate was El Pricko, my adrenalin did its work.

His beefy hand grasped the back of my tunic as I tried to slither past him groping for the light switch I'd remembered seeing.

With a brutal yank, he bounced me off his chest then his arms enveloped me in a crushing bear hug. The pain was excruciating. He exhaled his vile breath in my face. I didn't dare bite or scratch, the brute would kill me. Kicking his shins would only hurt my toes. It was hopeless to try for my hair spray. I made my body go limp. I moaned.

"Okay, kid. Okay, Gerta, we'll have some fun."

He lugged me towards the door apparently feeling for the light switch himself. The next minute, we were standing under the blaze of the ceiling light bulb.

I kept my head down and made sickening cooing, mewing sounds that I hope implied acquiescence or at least cooperation. By the force of my thoughts, I tried to will the brute to relax. I had to escape from the bondage of his arms.

"We're gonna have a good time—you'll see."

El Pricko was well-named. When his amorous inclinations caused his huge apparatus to rise to the occasion, I almost panicked. I arched my body away from him as though we were playing London Bridge.

One arm moved and he forced his grubby index finger under my chin and tried to raise my head. Finally, I let him succeed. I looked directly into the light and gave him a good look at my crinkly face.

I caught another expulsion of his horrid breath. This time it sounded as though I'd punched him in the diaphragm.

"Did you know," I spoke in dulcet tones, "that I am The Marshal's grandmother?"

Shock was clear on his face but I saw doubt as well, and anger. He released me and didn't move in the seconds it took me to open the door, slam it behind me and run down the hall. I flew down the stairs making contact with about three steps. Careening to the right, I opened the door opposite the bedroom with the snake poster. I remembered it was a closet. With the door closed, I silently pleaded with the deities who watch over addlepated old ladies.

El Pricko's heavy tread came down the stairs and stopped. I imagined fire and smoke shooting out of his hairy nostrils as he stood there raging at the fates that had let a fornication party slip through his fingers twice in one night. Were his delicate sensibilities outraged at the vision of my lived-in face? Maybe grandmother was overdoing it. The Marshal had to be fifty. But I was sure anyone over forty looked like Methuselah to El Pricko.

Attempting to reading El Pricko's mind occupied my thoughts. Why bother to find me? If I were The Marshal's grandmother, it could spell trouble. When his footsteps went quickly downstairs, I interpreted it as a decision to find Gerta and get on with his project.

Poor Gerta. I wondered what she looked like. What a horrible life she must lead being pursued by El Pricko whether she was upside down or right side up.

In the dark closet, I made space for myself to squat down and tried to regain my composure. Don't stay too long, I warned myself, or some common sense may infiltrate and persuade me to run home.

Reassured by the silence around me, I made an effort to leave my hiding place. I rearranged my cramped position and suddenly was terrified. A snake-like sinuous body moved down from above and settled around my shoulders. I could only think of the malevolent eyes of the boa constrictor on the poster. Something cool slid into my lap. I imagined his glistening spade-shaped head. The pump I'd relied on all these years felt like a football in my chest. My mouth was dry. Was I having a heart attack? The body slipped from my shoulders and coiled itself around my knee and leg.

Afraid I would faint, caution forgotten, I scrambled to my feet, wrenched the door open, and literally fell into the hall.

Strong arms caught me.

"Look out, sister." A brawny Ringer moved me away from the closet door. "I need this."

He bent over, reaching into the closet. I turned away. I did not want to watch.

"Oops, sorry," he said as he hit my legs. "Trying to get the mice out of the springs of my Porsche." I watched him disappear down the stairs, the vacuum cleaner's hose around his neck.

Finally satisfied that I was alone, I took a moment to congratulate myself on my grandmother play. It gave me more assurance when I went back upstairs and inspected the rest of the rooms on the third floor. Most of the doors were open or ajar and the rooms were empty. The second floor would be a riskier proposition but there was no point in delaying.

A mirror made me stop and remove some pine twigs from my hair. I arranged sticky strands of the mousy-colored stuff to almost hide my face. Muttering words of encouragement to myself, I went down the stairs, turning this time towards The Marshal's office.

Smoke wafted out of the room, the place was crowded with milling Ringers. No one noticed when I peeked in, it was so smoky they probably couldn't see me. Most of the Ringers were standing around a table eating cake. Empty Pepperidge Farm boxes were spilling over the top of the trash basket. Cans of drinks were on another table. Through the long distance part of my glasses I was able to conclude that Mountain Dew was the big favorite. The Marshal, with his back to me, puffing on a long black cigar, was on the phone. A couple of Ringers were standing in front of my painting. One of them, no doubt pointing out its faults, made me want to march in a tell him to keep his fingers to himself.

My costume definitely passed muster because two or three people passed me coming in and out of the doorway and seemed unaware of my existence.

Leaving the cake eaters, I went to the front bedroom I believed belonged to The Marshal, not that I expected to find Lew in there, but a clue to his fate might be anyplace.

I looked around the slightly open door. There were two figures in the four poster bed. I couldn't tell whether they were men or women or one of each. They appeared to be wrestling.

Tiptoeing to the next room, I carefully opened the door and witnessed the same kind of activity in an identical four poster, except in this case there were three participants.

The occupants of the next room held me spellbound. Light from the open bathroom door lit the stage. I'm not a voyeur and I equate Peeping Toms with vermin, but I had to stop and watch for a moment to make sure my old spectacles were working.

I realized that sexual practices had changes enormously since I used to neck in a rumble seat, but standing on your head!

Something brushed the back of my neck. I snapped around frightened that El Pricko had found me again and was relieved to find two mild-looking bearded Ringers. They too were mesmerized by the scene in the bedroom.

"I mean, like wow!"

The other one poked my wretched ribs with his elbow.

"Like, what are we waiting for?"

He put his hand on my back.

"I could hold her up and ... "

I didn't wait to hear the details of the game plan. I said something like 'see you later' and swiftly departed down to the back hall.

I opened the first door I came to and shuddered with relief when I found it was empty. The faint light from the window fell on a sewing machine, a few chairs and some bolts of home spun. I noticed a narrow door at the back. I had my hand on the knob when I heard the eager beavers in the next room trying to find me.

If they, no doubt, succeeded, I could be a grandmother again, but I had a feeling they wouldn't keep the news of The Marshal's grandmother to themselves. If I wasn't careful, I might have the whole hopped-up bunch running after me.

"Maybe she's in here."

I opened the small door so fast they couldn't possibly have seen me leave. Suddenly I was on my back, moving rapidly. My swift descent was so dramatic and so painful that it took a long time to realize that my position, lying down with my legs raised, was not due to hospital rules but because I was cushioned by crumbled towels and sheets in a big canvas laundry trolley.

Clearly I had sailed past the first floor and came to rest in the basement laundry and for the moment I wasn't planning to move.

14

"Are you new here?"

My first reaction to the question was to feel my head to make sure my wig was in place. Was it possible I'd fallen asleep in my comfy crib, or, overwhelmed by exhaustion, had I passed out? Either way, I realized I was emerging from an other-worldly condition.

The drab middle-aged woman asked another question. "Why are you doing the laundry this time of night?"

Was this how the Ringers did their laundry? I mumbled something unintelligible and tried to climb out of the trolley.

"Guess I had too much to drink". I reinforced my confession by crossing my eyes. I think she believed me when I groaned in agony as I forced my ribs over the metal rim of the trolley. I wondered if there was a world record on how many times you could break your ribs and still survive.

Unzipping my pocket, I folded my hand around the can of hair spray. After what I had been through, I wasn't intimidated by this passive creature, but I didn't want to take a chance. Who knows what was going on in her head as she stood staring at me.

"Where is Lew Weber?" I tried.

She looked blank. I asked her again. And, did she have the key to his room? Still no response.

"Do you know Phoebe?" She continued to stare at me. "Do you know where I can find Phoebe's Knee?"

With her arm stretched behind her, she backed towards the door. Discouraged, I crossed my eyes again. Before she made her exit, I leaned and grabbed her arm. "Don't tell anybody about me doing the laundry tonight, please. It's a surprise."

Almost imperceptably, the harsh lines that bracketed her mouth softened. Maybe it was her turn to do the laundry and I was relieving her of some work.

She departed closing the door behind her. Instantly, I checked to see if it was locked. Thank goodness I wasn't destined to do time in the laundry—there was no lock.

A closet along one wall was full of Ringers' robes. Another larger closet was full of civilian garments - regular street clothes, pants, jackets, whole suits. I didn't take time to examine them carefully but registered surprise as I kicked assorted footgear on the floor. Perhaps the Ringers were too thrifty to cast away the props of a past life.

The role of laundress seemed like a good disguise so when I went to explore the rest of the basement, I carried a pillow case full of towels.

Getting into the room behind the laundry was a cinch. The door wasn't locked and there were no Ringers prowling around to interrupt me. The place looked like a car repair shop. Parts of dismantled engines were on the floor. A long work bench held tools, oil cans, fan belts, exhaust pipes and piles of nuts and bolts. It looked more like a place to tinker than a serious business because, of course, there weren't any cars.

I wondered if parts of Lew's Volvo were right in front of me. Maybe the Ringers had time on their hands and, like the poor fellow with mice in his Porsche, liked to keep their cars in perfect condition. Only so much time could be spent tending the greenhouses. Whatever they grew—and I was sure it was marijuana—had to have time to grow.

The only other door in the basement seemed to be locked. I twisted the knob slowly at first, then impatiently. Before I could get the credit card out of my pocket, the door opened and a man in sweat pants and an undershirt peered out at me.

"What d'ya want?" His delivery was pugnacious.

It was clear my interruption was unwelcome. The putty knife held in his dirty hand looked threatening. "Who are you? What d'ya want?"

With sudden inspiration I told him I was Phoebe. "Would you like to see Phoebe's knee?"

"Are you crazy, lady? I'm busy. Go away."

It was impossible to see any part of the room behind him. I leaned against the door.

"I'm Lew Weber's mother. Do you know where I can find Lew?"

Clearly disgusted, he tried to close the door.

"I want to pick up his laundry." I flashed what I hoped was a winning smile. "I'll do yours, too."

"Please go away, lady." The door closed followed by the click of its lock.

Trudging back to the laundry, I sat down and tried to analyze my unsuccessful meeting with the abrupt, rude Ringer. The man's irritation at being interrupted struck me as being genuine. His attitude didn't seem to be suspicious. He didn't act like the cautious guardian of a prisoner.

Eventually I convinced myself that Lew wasn't

being held in the room. I had to resist a temptation to crawl back into the dirty laundry bin and pretend the whole miserable evening was a dream.

From visits to Amber Trees in years past, I knew that the rooms on the first floor were on a grand scale, hardly a place to hide a prisoner, but I intended to walk through them to assure myself that I had conducted a thorough search of Amber Trees.

Some creature, eating celery, had his head and shoulders in the fridge as I walked through the kitchen. The ornate dining room was empty. A black marble mantle supported by voluptuous alabaster maidens made the rest of the room seem sordid. It was used as a mess hall, with saw horses topped with sheets of plywood serving as dining tables. Stackable metal chairs leaned against the carved dado. Where brocade draperies had once hung, worn window shades were pulled to uneven lengths. Exposed wires were capped on the ceiling where a crystal chandelier had once hung.

Oh well, I wasn't here to record the decline of elegance. I really didn't give a damn whether they had draperies or shades, or nothing. I just wanted to find Lew and get out of the scary, depressing place.

I pushed the swinging door into what used to be called the morning room. Now it was used as a dormitory. A few beds were occupied. Two explosive snorers were painfully out of sync. I turned away from the dreary sound.

Back in the dining room I looked through a slit in the heavy curtains. The cavernous living room was dark. At the far end there was a flicker of light I couldn't identify. My eyes, adjusting to the darkness, soon confirmed what my other senses had warned me—that the room was full of people. I slipped through the curtains, holding them closed behind me.

"And this," a voice announced, "is the last one."

A color slide flashed on the white wall. It was a picture I had seen before. Bewildered, I gazed at a photograph of the stone chamber at South Woodstock.

Lights came on, and about fifteen Ringers stood up, making a racket as they folded and stacked their chairs. No one noticed me.

I touched the arm of an innocuous looking young man.

"I was late. The laundry, you know." I waggled my hands as though they were wet. "What other slides did he show?"

"Rocks." He tapped his forehead with his finger. "It's rocks in the head he's got."

"Was the whole show about rocks?"

"Naw, just a couple of pictures."

Framing another question, I realized my boy was backing away from me. Alarms rang in my head. Would he report a stranger? Carefully he folded his chair, stretched, scratched and sauntered off with a companion.

I wasn't accustomed to rejection but the expression of distaste on his face made it clear that a stringy-haired bespectacled old witch in dirty sweat pants and a rumpled tunic was not his cup of tea.

With my back turned to the room, I bustled around straightening up the stacks of chairs and tried, with no luck, to catch any comments about the slide show.

Tall French doors opening onto the porch looked like an ideal exit. I wanted to scream when they refused to open. I could see but not reach slip bolts holding the door closed at the top. The sight of Ringers gathering on the front porch made me decide to leave Amber Trees the way I had entered.

Walking boldly by a couple talking in the kitchen, I almost ran out the door. My relief was so intense I felt sick. For a minute I hugged a slim tree to keep my knees from wobbling.

Once outside the oblong of light, I made my way to the tiny cellar windows which I hoped would give me a look at the hostile Ringer's workshop. Lying on my stomach, I tried to rub a peep hole on the filthy glass. My efforts were futile. I decided the windows were covered on the inside.

An arm placed across my back made me freeze in icy terror. I didn't have the stamina to face another encounter. I felt perilously close to feeling like a victim, which I knew would be fatal.

A whisper told me to lie still and be quiet. A gentle whisper, not a command. The whisperer pressed close to my side and squeezed my shoulder.

It couldn't be El Pricko, thank God. The touch was light. I tried to turn away and get on my hands and knees.

"Tish, it's me. It's okay."

Close to hysteria I laughed out loud. My nickname for Kay was 'Okay'. She shushed me again.

"They've locked the gates. I had to find you. I've been so worried. Are you all right?"

Kay moved away far enough for me to get her in focus. Her hair, unpinned, fell over her shoulders. Her monk's cloth tunic was torn down the front and her lip was bleeding. She dabbed at it with the back of her hand.

"The smelly bald baboon. I'm going to have him castrated if it's the last thing I ever do."

"Did he . . . ?"

"He tried. We can't talk now. Gotta get out of here. When that ape can walk again, he's going to come looking for me."

I told her his name. Kay wasn't too enthusiastic about my description of our alternate escape route under the fence. The very thought of it made me want to cry. Struggling through a half a mile of woods seemed insurmountable.

"Wait a minute." The stage whisper came from the side porch. We couldn't see anyone but the urgency of his words was unmistakable. "Listen."

We stood clutching each other like nymphs trapped in a mural.

"Mrs. McWhinny. You all right?"

My heart nearly exploded.

"Lew Weber!"

"Quiet, quiet. Yes, it's Luke Wedder."

I started to speak when he stopped me. I could see his hand now held up in warning and a pale bit of face behind it.

"Listen carefully. Don't tell anyone you've seen me. It's terribly important. It's vital." He repeated it. "Not a soul, don't tell a single soul. Have you been to Phoebe's Knee?"

In a voice too loud I asked him about Phoebe's Knee.

"Where is it, what is it, who . . . ?"

"Up behind here", he pointed toward the mountain. "It's dangerous, don't tell . . . "

One of the French doors opened. The light fell on two figures and instantly they both disappeared inside the building.

"Let's find him," I pulled at Kay, then changed my mind.

135

"You stay here. I've got to talk to him."

My tunic tore as Kay grabbed it trying to stop me.

Ringers were still on the front porch, some of them sitting on the steps. They were passing around weeds, each smoker holding the joint between thumb and index finger, some with pinkies raised daintily, all of them taking long drags of the sweet smoke.

Maybe I should have joined them, it was tempting, instead of walking between them, It took my last ounce of courage to approach the stairs. Inhaling deeply, I marched up the stairs.

One of them tugged the hem of my tunic. I was afraid the whole thing would fall off.

"Hey, do I know you?"

"I'm his grandmother." I pointed towards the house.

"Whose grandmother?"

The Marshal's name silenced him, but they all turned to watch me walk through the door.

I felt time running out like a wave from a sand castle. The thought of meeting a further enraged El Pricko terrified me. My cool determination had wilted. A telephone in the front hall made me want to dial Hilary's familiar number and yell, "Help, come get me."

Pressed against the wall, I lowered my head and let three people pass by. A tall Ringer closest to me took my wrist in an excrutiatingly painful grip. He inclined his head. Between clenched teeth he said two words. "Get out."

15

"I can't go any further." Hanging onto the fence I reminded myself of Scarlett a few days ago, but I had no energy left and I couldn't possible have shaken the fence. Kay had suggested climbing over it, but with a closer look at me, she didn't push the idea.

She led the way uphill, staying close to the fence where those installing it had stamped down the underbrush. Often she stopped to take my hand to pull me along. Without her, I'd still be standing in the shadow of Amber Trees, drained of vitality and unable to make a decision.

Kay let me sit on a log for a few minutes to collect enough energy to propel me up the next hill. We were struggling up the shoulder of Lofty Mountain, to call it a hill was misleading. Even Kay, young and athletic, looked exhausted.

The euphoria of finding Lew, or whatever his name was, had passed with the conundrum of his role as a Ringer. Kay had sense enough to restrain her curiosity about my adventures. She could see I was on the brink of collapse.

She massaged my back between my shoulder blades. Even her soothing touch hurt.

She pulled me to my feet. "Come on, you crazy spy, let's go."

When finally we came to the back fence, I paused

to check with the deities who were supposed to be taking care of me. Thanks were in order. I felt like the last marathoner to cross the line.

"We need Cootie Razor."

"The hell with Cootie. Just give me your flashlight again, Tish. I'll find the darn place."

"If you walk close enough to the fence, you'll fall in it."

Which is just what Kay did about five minutes later. In the darkness she looked like a shaggy dog digging a hole. The ditch on the upland side of the fence was adequate though still covered with leaves, but it had been difficult for me to reach the Ringer side of the fence with my trowel. Kay had to clear out at least another four cubic feet of earth. Her curses sounded like Lulu growling.

She sat back on her haunches, rubbing her hands.

"This will have to do. Think I've hit ledge and my fingers are worn down to the knuckle."

We discussed the best way to tackle our exit. Kay insisted on going first.

"There's more of me than you. If I can get through, so can you. I'll have to go under on my back, no way I could bend in the other direction." She hugged her chest. "Wish me luck."

A million old movies flashed through my mind featuring prison escapes. Any moment I expected the whine of sirens, spotlights sweeping the woods and the angry baying of guard dogs.

Kay managed to get her head and shoulders under the fence. With her knees bent, she pushed and wiggled slowly moving by inches. Her hips were her largest dimension but at least they were tough and could take the treatment she was giving them.

Describing her excess flesh with horrible obscenities, Kay struggled back. The opening had to be larger. I took my turn digging. Gleefully, I told Kay I'd remembered my knife. We could make quick work of the packed earth that had to be removed.

She said some other shocking things about the condition of the world when I removed my hands from my pockets and showed them to her empty.

I'm lucky, I thought, as I scratched at the earth, that a Swiss army knife is all that I lost tonight.

On the next try, Kay almost cleared the fence when her pants became enmeshed with the wire.

It was then that I saw them. First I saw one, then three more walking behind.

I held Kay's ankles. "Don't move or you'll be very sorry."

Kay snorted with impatience. "Let go, for Pete's sake. I'm fine now."

"Just shut up and don't move."

She had the sense to respond to the urgency in my voice.

"What's the matter?" she whispered.

They were walking single file, the largest one, on all fours, nudged her tangled hair. I warned Kay again not to move quickly and to speak softly. Then I described the group fanning out around her head.

A gorgeous, stylish mother skunk and her chic but chubby children were inspecting Kay's hair with obvious pleasure. I had to hold my ribs when I laughed, watching mother skunk touch Kay's cheek with her black nose. The children followed suit. Kay was transfixed. The whites of her eyes were enormous.

Mother skunk must have decided that Kay wasn't

portable, probably not edible, and clearly not playful, so the storybook quartet disappeared into the night.

Our next visitors weren't as silent. We stopped laughing.

Kay, extricated from the trough, crawled into a pine thicket. "Hide, Tish. Sounds like a damn army."

Hoping to look like an old stump, I turned my back, lowered my head and leaned against a tree trunk.

Light from a powerful torch played along the fence. There was terrible commotion in the woods and a man's gravelly voice. "Oh, no. Oh, God damn, she got hit."

There was more thrashing and another voice cried out, "I've been hit, too."

I turned in time to see a huge animal bound out of the woods and throw himself at the fence. In the next second I recognized my floppy-eared friend, Cootie.

Tears of joy ran down my dirty face as Cootie licked my fingers through the fence. She then discovered Kay and slathered her with kisses. Clyde appeared, and aimed his light at Kay then directed the beam in my face.

"Well, there you are, Ma'am."

Hilary, a foot taller than Clyde, loomed up behind him. His churlish tome revealed his anxiety.

"Tish, you damned fool, you okay?"

Not waiting for a reply, he helped me under the fence.

"Gently, Hil, gently. My ribs are like macaroni. My Lord, did you bring the skunks with you?"

For the first time I realized that fresh skunk juice smelled like crushed garlic. That explained why, unlike most people, I had never considered skunk smell obnoxious.

The men hustled us out of the woods. Hilary supported me with my arm held firmly through his. Cootie, Clyde and Kay ran interference. Ten minutes later, Lulu's bark was the loveliest sound I had ever heard.

Hilary refused to pollute my house in his present condition and stayed on the porch. With Lulu in my lap, I collapsed into a cushioned wicker rocking chair. Clyde and Cootie sat on the front steps. He rubbed her loose skin.

"Pole cat really got you, old girl," he smiled. "I think she likes the smell."

Kay appeared clutching a bottle of cognac and a stack of small glasses.

Clyde drank his in one gulp. I took a sip. "Here's to being alive and—" I almost said something about finding Lew. Could I keep that news from Hilary? Being basically an open person, the prospect of keeping Lew's whereabouts was going to tax my character. Not that I couldn't keep a secret. In fact, I was an excellent choice as a confidant because I usually forgot what I had been told. Decisions were for tomorrow.

Kay drank her cognac and refilled her glass. "Death to El Pricko."

Hilary wasn't listening. He asked us rather pathetically, "What'll I do, take a bath in tomato juice?"

"Wait a minute." Kay went in the house and returned with an old trench coat of Doug's. Take your clothes off. We won't look. Give them to me, I'll give them the treatment. Ammonia and five times around in Tish's washer."

Clyde got up to leave, apparently not curious about

141

why Kay and I were crawling under the fence in the middle of the night. Or more likely, he was thoughtful and sensitive to my condition and had the patience to wait for an explanation. He departed with his happy malodorous hound.

"Phew," Kay said. "The dog smells worse than you do, Hilary."

I explained that Cootie had brought a very potent smell of her own and the marriage of smells had brought out the worst of both. I asked Hilary how he knew where I was and how he had found us.

"Cootie found you, but to begin with, I stopped here on the way back from the Inn, brought you a lobster claw. When you weren't here, I had a strong suspicion you'd gone to Amber Trees but I couldn't see myself just walking in. Might spoil your act or something. I went to the gates anyhow, and they'd just closed them. I think I saw you, Kay, running across the lawn. Knew you'd have to get out of there. So I went to the Inn and called Clyde. Thank God he answered and he came right over. Think he's got a crush on you, Tish. Well, you know the rest."

Hilary wanted to know what happened at Amber Trees. I shook my head. Tomorrow, I promised.

"How did you know," I asked Kay, "that I had gone to Amber Trees?"

She told us that the day of our trip to Boston she sensed I had nefarious plans and was worried about me. She saw me emerge with a package from the joke store and later had no trouble finding out from the owner what I had bought. The explanation brought a flood of joy. The wig, she said, had given her the important clues—and this morning with the Marshall she sensed my search for Lew was reaching a dangerous pitch. She came to Lofton at dusk—watched my house fruitlessly—and about ten o'clock, went to Amber Trees herself. She had rigged up a costume that let her pass as a Ringer. She said the gate was unguarded. She snooped around looking in windows. El Pricko jumped her on a side porch. He was so powerful and he smelled so awful and the noises he made were so repulsive, she said, that she was transformed into a wildcat.

When he had her pinned to the wall and grabbed at his fly zip, she bit his arm. When he drew back to hit her, she drove her knee into his crotch. He twirled around clutching himself, Kay said. She gave him a push, his back hit the porch railing, he lost his balance and toppled over into the juniper bushes. Then she found me.

I used the last bit of energy I had to clap my hands. With still a sip in my glass I seconded Kay's toast.

"Death to El Pricko."

"You know," Hilary said, "if I was that guy I'd be mad."

He rose, looking like the senior lead in a bathhouse comedy.

"Be sure the doors are locked. Tish, you've got a gun, put it by your bed. Lulu will let you know if he comes."

He turned with his hand on the car door. "You didn't find the boy, did you?"

Kay answered for me. "We did not find Lew Weber."

The was the specious kind of lying that I hated the most, but I was grateful for the kind spirit that made her spare me telling a more direct lie.

We watched him drive off and with wordless agreement closed up the house and went upstairs.

Kay settled down in the room next to mine. She left the door open.

I wondered if one could drown by falling asleep in the bathtub. The answer must be no, because I did come out, half an hour later, limp as Raggedy Ann. Wrapped in a thick terry cloth robe, I padded into Kay's room to say goodnight.

Looking cozy in bed with her arm around Lulu, Kay asked, "Did he say Luke Hebber?"

"Something like that." I shrugged. "No wonder no one has ever heard of Lew Weber. Ain't no such person. I'm so utterly confused, can't think tonight."

I picked up Lulu, who clearly had planned to spend the night with Kay. I put her on my bed and got out my gun. Doug's gun, actually. I hate the darn things. It was a small caliber revolver. I knew enough to check the chambers. I had fired it a couple of times, and felt I could manage to do so again.

But shoot at a person? Flesh and blood? Even El Pricko? I wondered if I could. In bed, I tried to imagine situations in which I would shoot at smoeone and realized there could be plenty of causes. If I saw El Pricko walk into Kay's room—sure I'd shoot him. If he tried to steal Lulu, I'd shoot him. That's why hand guns should be banned, I reflected. There were plenty of times when you might use them.

What a dear friend Kay had been, and a brave one. How could I have doubted her that day in Boston? It took courage to storm Amber Trees. And what if she hadn't overcome El Pricko? It made me sick to think how close to catastrophe my search for Lew had brought her.

No matter what Lew's mission was, or for what reason he vowed us to silence, at least I knew he was alive and seemed to be in control of his own destiny.

My interest in him now would be simply old-fashioned curiosity.

The light was still on in Kay's room.

"In case you want to know what I'm going to do tomorrow, Kay, I'll tell you. I'm going to spend the entire day in bed."

There was a moment of silence and then Kay appeared in one of my old flannel nightgowns. Her arms akimbo, she frowned down at me.

"Oh, no, you're not, Madame. Tomorrow, as you seem to have forgotten, is the opening of your exhibition."

16

Vermonters forget rain, mud, ice and slush when they describe a crisp clear day in September as a typical Vermont day. Double checking my Swatch, I found it hard to believe it was ten o'clock. When had I last slept that late? Possibly in Madrid in the sixties, after I had adjusted to dinner at eleven or twelve at night.

One of the reasons I had slept so long was clear when I saw the telephone receiver off the hook in the study. Kay's handiwork. A note said she expected me at the gallery at four and that Hilary had invited us for supper after the opening.

There was a note tucked under my door. Hilary had to go to Brattleboro but would meet me at the gallery. In a way I was glad we couldn't drive over together. As much as I wanted to talk to him, I felt sure I'd break my word and tell him about Lew. Hilary knew me so well, he'd sense I was holding something back if I didn't tell him.

With breakfast in mind, I found that there was no skim milk in the fridge, so I pulled on jeans, sneakers and a sweat shirt and, with Lulu, walked over to the store. Marge and Kevin were busy waiting on customers, most of whom I knew. I had a feeling of walking into a world that had gone on turning without me. Wasn't my hellish night with the Ringers written in the wrinkles of my face?

Sidling over, I looked at myself in the metal mirror attached to a card displaying dark glasses. I looked the same. "Hey!" I wanted to shatter the scene's amicable complacency. "Hey! Do you know I spent the night leaping around with all those dangerous fornicating pot-heads at Amber Trees? And look, here I am, a survivor."

"Penny for your thoughts." Kevin strightened the display. He didn't really want to know my thoughts. He wanted to tell me about the roast beef that had just been delivered. "It's really rare, the way you like it. Want some?"

Suddenly famished, I watched him slice a half a pound of beef. The first paper thin slice was for Lulu, who expected Kevin's generosity and stood with her front paws against his leg. Along with the milk, thin rye bread and a fist of bibb lettuce completed my errands.

Charlie Reed, in his becoming trooper's uniform, took the paper bag from my arms and held open the screen door.

"That's a new one." He pointed to the dog we both had to step over. Lulu walked around the sleeping behemoth. "I guess once there were more cows than people in Lofton. Now it's dogs."

As we walked to my house, I considered my problem. How could I tell Charlie about Phoebe's Knee and about seeing the slide of the South Woodstock rock chamber without revealing my lawless activities of the night?

Spreading a mixture of horseradish and mayonnaise on the bread, I told Charlie I had reason to believe that Phoebe's Knee might be a cave or a chamber. A few days ago when he heard that Phoebe was the name of Lew Weber's grandmother's pug, he had lost interest in the significance of the rock message. I think Charlie was genuinely fond of me but thought I was a little crazy.

I went on to tell him that this cave or chamber was up behind Amber Trees. I lied and told him the information came from The Marshal. He seemed satisfied with my lame explanation and even expressed enthusiasm for a search party to comb the woods.

In reply to a question from me about the undesirables in Lofton, Charlie said that although there were more people coming in and out of Amber Trees and the farms, tough looking people, nothing illegal had occurred, and there was no reason to apprehend anyone.

Marijuana was on my mind, but I hesitated to ask him about the greenhouses. I didn't want to get involved in any discussion about the Ringers. I regretted bringing up the topic. Lew might be endangered if I did any more meddling.

Almost unconsciously, I had accepted the idea that Lew had intended to infiltrate the Ring of Right, but I had nagging doubts. Had he joined the cult for some ulterior purpose? Money? Power? Could he possibly believe in the pursuit of whatever demon they worshipped?

Leaving Charlie the trooper's concerns and switching to Charlie the archaeologist's favorite subject, we discussed the possibility of chambers on Lofty Mountain.

Chambers or temples were usually built on high land, though none had been found on a mountain side. But in the foot hills of Lofty behind our houses, he felt, there were logical sites. Portals of the structure would face in the right direction for a proper astronomical alignment to observe the summer solstice.

"What we want to look for is a large pointed stone, like the summer solstice monolith at Mystery Hill," a site which Charlie described as America's Stonehenge. "Or, instead of the sunset pinpointed on the top of a rock at the exact moment of the solstice, we mught find the sun precisely framed in the V-shape made by a couple of faraway hills or mountains."

Charlie stayed in a state of suspended animation while I answered a phone call from Kay. Taking a break from work, she wanted to discuss our meeting with Lew.

"Make yourself another sandwich, Charlie. Be with you in a moment."

"The law is visiting you," she guessed. "Have you told him anything about last night or about Fatso Smith's near miss with his maker?"

My negative reply made Kay express her doubts.

"Maybe you should, Tish. Something tells me there might be trouble."

Trouble, I agreed, was possible, but what could Charlie do? I saw him as an eager youngster, an exemplary Eagle Scout, an apt pupil of archeology, but not as a knowledgable firm-handed officer of the law. My inclination was to let things ride. I'd make quick work of the portrait. I'd try to honor Lew's request and let time do its usual work.

When Charlie left, I planned my trip to Manchester. A twenty minute drive meant nothing to me usually, but my ribs required attention. I dug out a disgraceful old quilted coat. It might soften the impact of the cold vinyl seat in the station wagon and insulate me against Lulu. The sight of another dog by the roadside or in a passing car threw her into a frenzy. She'd fly through the wagon like an olympic hurdler, frequently crashing into me.

An apricot jersey dress seemed a cheerful choice for the opening. I shampooed my hair and worked on my nails. A painter's work leaves you out of the running as a model for a Revlon advertisement. A niece had sent me a pair of lace stockings which I hoped would distract my friends' attention from my weary face. For the same reason I polished my glasses which graduated to a smoky color at the top, a style that did a lot for those of us who had racked up a lot of mileage around the eyes.

This exhibition had required no work on my part. It was made up of watercolors painted during the last few years. Kay had collected them from racks and drawers around my studio. She took care of mat cutting and framing. It was a relief to have her now as my sole agent. It gave me time to paint and not concern myself with the mechanics of selling.

Her job included doing almost everything, except the actual painting or drawing. For her efforts she made a fifty percent commission on everything I sold. A usual agent's fee, though Kay said the fee was higher in New York. It was her effort that placed my paintings before juries for group shows. Such exhibitions removed thirty percent of the selling price. Kay didn't add her commission on those occasions, as she considered the exposure good advertising.

One of her duties which I appreciated the most had to do with pricing my paintings, she told the sitters what their portraits would cost. The less I knew about that end of the business, the happier I was. Without her I'd probably still be painting for pennies. A reliable indication of old age is when you think everything costs too much. The prices she charged for my work made me gasp.

After a nap and a bracing mug of tea, I left for Manchester. Once a charming small village, it lately had seemed to confuse progress with change. Once, one could mosey in and out of pleasant low-key shops, nodding and smiling at familiar faces. Now, a favorite emporium could vanish overnight, almost unremarked. The Quality Restaurant still prospers, though unrecognizable, under new management, its cozy booths banished, rock music blaring. It was there friends used to meet after a shopping spree or a trip to the dentist. A turreted outlet store on the main corner in town looks as though it's trying to push route eleven into the Battenkill. MacDonald's and Friendly's have moved in, along with other chain operations that are irrevocably turning a once homey stretch of road into a characterless copy of a thousand other streets in America.

The Anderson Art Gallery parking lot was behind the small Vermont Gothic building. Three exhibition rooms fitted comfortably on the first floor. Above, Kay lived in two large bright rooms. She rented the top floor apartment. The small plot of grass beside the house was where Kay had said she intended to build a rock chamber.

I struggled out of my coat and left it in the car. Kay wouldn't like having to introduce the artist as Humpty Dumpty.

Hilary greeted me at the door with a glass of champagne.

"Ugh. Did you pay for this sparkling bath suds?"

Speechless, I stared. Hilary was distinguished-looking in any company but today he looked sensational.

151

"Look, my pretty, take a look." He revolved in a circle inviting my scrutiny. "Want to paint me?"

"Your Van Dyke, was that for cosmetic reasons all these years? Did you want to look narrow? Why didn't you tell me that under those whiskers you were hiding a magnificent square chin? Of course I want to paint you."

Massaging his jaw, Hilary beamed. "The prospect of smelling like a skunk every rainy day for the rest of my life drove me to the blade. You coming back to my place?"

There was just time to say yes before I was swept away by some exuberant friends. An hour later, still greeting people, I was perched on a stool which Kay had provided.

An hour after that I had my feet up on a worn leather hassock at Hilary's. My ribs firmly held by the canvas back of a campaign chair. A Scotch as dark as tea was never far from my lips.

Circled by a screen porch, Hilary's house reminded me of a lakeside cabin. Inside, the living room and kitchen had been turned into one big messy room. Stacks of newspapers and magazines served as an end table for the old leather couch. An empty wire spool, courtesy of Central Vermont Public Service, made a capacious coffee table. There were a couple of Navajo rugs, two worn canvas sling chairs and a long dining table which was used as a desk when Hilary wasn't entertaining.

He described the bookshelves that took up every bit of wall space as his insulation. The first blender Fred Waring ever made was his prized possession and a tangle of wires led to every other kind of kitchen gadget that had been made since, including the latest model Cuisinart and a juice extractor that looked like the Empire State Building. If I could give a darn about kitchens, I would have felt the lack of counter space, since every flat surface was covered with pots and pans and bowls. There was no "space".

They say that old age is a time when you do too many things for the last time and too few for the first time. Today was the last time, I told Kay, that I was going to stand up for three hours at the opening of an exhibition of mine. But, I said to myself, illegal entry and trespassing were new experiences for me. Maybe if I could keep the scales balanced I could hold off the lavender and old lace a little longer.

Hilary was cooking, with Lulu in attendance. Not only did he like to have her to keep the floor tidy, he muttered about his culinary effort and asked rhetorical questions. "Where's the pepper, Lulu?" as though she'd know. Or, "Now let's turn this darn thing over, shall we? The plates, let's see, Tish, Kay, maybe Terry, Walter and Scarlett. And me. Six, right?"

"Are we going to tell them about last night, Tish?" It was Kay speaking quietly.

That was a hard decision, but we both agreed that for safety's sake it might be wise. Suppose El Pricko could identify us and lusted for revenge. It would be better if these few kind friends knew the background.

"Besides," Kay said, "What a giddy tale. I can dine out on this one all winter."

Terry did come, looking natty in a tattersal waistcoat. He brought a bag of brownies from the Inn.

Kay bragged that I had sold six water colors at the opening and Terry said he'd like her to manage him. I wondered what he had to sell aside from good looks and a medium portion of charm.

Admittedly, I was biased, not against Terry but for Walter, and while I usually paid little attention to

Kay's affairs of the heart, she had been mooning around lately and talking about having a baby. From her friends' experiences she decided single parenthood was not for her but she wanted more than a stud. A dilemma she shared with a zillion other attractive independent women who saw forty on the horizon.

Dusky bronze candelabra at either end of a scarred but handsome antique refectory table held candles that towered over the guests, bathing everyone in a flattering light.

Given a vote, I think Loftonites would choose dinner at Hilary's capacious table as the best act in town.

How he managed to extract such delectable food from the prodigious mess in his kitchen, probably only Lulu knew.

In no way did he resemble the cool hostess touted in magazine articles, who, with advance planning, made her dinner party seem effortless.

Hilary dropped pans, spilled vital ingredients and cut his hands or set fire to the potholders in a running series of catastrophes, none of which he endured in silence.

When he bellowed at us to sit down, no one dawdled. Though they'd never met, he'd been having a long term affair with cookbook genius Marcella Hazen so we didn't feel cheated when he said supper was just pasta and salad.

Hilary dished out generous portions of penne into basin-sized soup plates.

"Penne col sugo di Cavofiore," he announced. "For you Yankee illiterates that's cauliflower, anchovies, garlic, oil, some parsley and a little red pepper."

Exotic salad greens came from a Londonderry farm. Doused with Hil's Balsamic vinegar dressing, it

154

made you wish winter would never come. The French bread he had baked the day before. We could pour ourselves red or white wine.

Conversation was limited to our thoughts about food until Hilary served us decaffeinated coffee as rich and good as anything I'd drunk on the Rialto. The bottle of Amaretto he opened was unnecessary. We had all had more than enough to drink.

Hilary and I exchanged glances when Scarlett knocked over her wine glass. The wine ran in my direction, found an ancient worm hole and dripped on my foot.

Kay, always an asset at a dinner party, sopped up the wine with a sponge. She grinned at me. "Shall I begin?"

She held the guests spellbound as she began her saga with the mystery of seeing me emerge from a wig store in Boston. By the time she got to her battle with El Pricko, all three male diners had unconsciously assumued truculent poses. Walter held his butter knife like a dagger.

Hilary modestly accepted the praise of all when Kay described our thrilling, smelly rescue. Rubbing his smooth chin he said, "Now, Mata Hari, we'd like to hear from you."

Hilarious laughter greeted my description of sex life in Amber Trees. Even Scarlett was jogged out of her rather somber boozy mood when I told them about the upside-down lovers. An important episode I'd forgotten to tell them was about the slide show and the picture of the South Woodstock chamber. Subconsciously I must have avoided the subject because Phoebe's Knee and rock chambers came too close to revealing what Kay and I knew about Lew.

"Standing on their heads?" Walter leered at Kay. "Are you busy later?"

"Never you mind. I suggest you check in down the street."

"I'd be scared. Tish, how did you have the nerve to go barging in there?" He raised his glass. "Here's to a gutsy lady."

"A demented woman is more like it." Hilary added his opinion.

Neither Kay nor I mentioned seeing Lew, though everyone questioned us about him. Kay said she thought that if indeed he was with the Ringers, he was probably down at one of the farms. "How about it, Tish, shall we do a little exploring down there?"

Of course she was joking. My role as trespasser and unpopular investigator was over. Lew was on his own.

"Don't you dare," Terry said. "I went down to look around the other day, pretended to be lost, knocked on the door and asked for directions. They'd never even heard of the next town. They're mean-looking thugs. How do you know El Pricko isn't recuperating down there? Give the farms a wide, wide berth."

Scarlett asked me if I'd finished the portrait. Before leaving for Manchester, I'd called Amber Trees and made an appointment for eleven o'clock Monday.

"Tomorrow. I'm going to wrap it up tomorrow."

Shaking her head, she made no comment.

Hilary poured himself some Amaretto. "These Ringers are a horror and a curse. I'd give an awful lot to get them out of Lofton."

"Oh you would? How about a deal?" Walter asked. "If I can run the Ringers out of town, will you sell us your land on the mountain?"

"Don't count on buying my land. The whole lot of them will leave eventually. They'll break the law—or just get caught doing something rotten."

"But," Walter waggled his finger, "suppose the Ringers were to leave soon. Before, say, Thanksgiving. That's two months away. What would you say to that?"

Hilary smiled. "You do that fella, then we'll talk about my land."

Scarlett struck her Rubenesque chest with her fist. "I brought them to Lofton and I'll get them out of Lofton."

"The Marshal," Terry said, "appears to be the absolute ruler, like the guru that led everybody around by the nose in Oregon. If we could just do him in, maybe the whole lousy bunch would leave." He rose picking up his plate and wine glass.

Kay took them away, insisting that she was in charge of cleaning up. Walter got up, gathering some plates, and boasted about his outstanding qualification as a scullery slave.

Terry put his hands on Scarlett's shoulders and offered to drive her home.

I hitched a ride with them promising to call Hilary when I came back from Amber Trees tomorrow.

Each of the men in turn had gallantly offered to stand beside me while I finished the portrait. But being watched while I paint makes me nervous, and besides, there wasn't anything frightening about visiting Amber Trees in the daytime and at The Marshal's request.

17

A reason for eating pasta that hasn't been advertised is its importance as soul food. A pasta-lined tummy means a good night's sleep, at least for me. Add to that a case of exhaustion and a sense of relief about Lew's survival.

Work-day habits took over any lingering thoughts about Ringers, except for one. My sitter.

My broadly painted resemblance of him had the liveliness of most sketches. What the picture needed to become a successful informal portrait was rich red for his tunic and more intensity on the dark and light sides of his head.

It made me impatient waiting for eleven o'clock. Usually my portraits were on the easel in my studio where I could study them at my leisure.

A guardian near the gates to Amber Trees, busy trying to clean his fingernails with pine needles, ignored me. The same mousey Ringer opened the door to let me in. No one else was in the entry hall and the living room appeared to be empty. Sun streaming in the tall windows made my Saturday night experiences recede into an ugly musty memory.

The Marshal was having his morning snooze. Posed properly, his head was almost invisible under a copy of Barron's tabloid-size newspaper.

"He's asleep. I'll tell him you're here."

I stopped my doe-eyed guide. "Don't, please. There's a lot I can do while he's napping."

His hands held the pose on the arms of the wooden chair and the folds of his red tunic hid his porky form in elegant clerical folds. With no demands on my social behavior, I concentrated on painting.

Squeezing globs of vermilion, cadmium red and alizarin crimson was a joy, but nothing compared to the pleasure of applying it on the canvas with a flexible palette knife.

Long verticals of vermilion began to bring the painting to life. My sitter was sinking deeper and deeper into sleep. A toad, that's what he looked like, a toad in a red jumper.

Stretching and deep breathing after an hour of work delivered the oxygen for another half hour. My model's chunky hands needed some cool shadows and his gold watch deserved a fleck of lemon yellow for a highlight. His golden phallus was hidden in a fold of his tunic.

Voices from the hall penetrated my absorption. With the slight hope that one of the speakers might be Lew, I put my palette on a chair and opened the door.

Three Ringers with their backs turned toward me continued to talk as they walked to the stairs. None of them was tall.

With no one in sight and The Marshal asleep I couldn't resist taking a look at the sewing room down the hall. It seemed so improbable that I could have fallen down a laundry chute, I wanted to see just how it may have happened.

With the poise and speed of an accomplished thief, I slipped through the door, closing it behind me.

Examining the door of the laundry chute, I heard

feet pounding down the hall. I opened the door a crack, and listened to voices echoing a sense of urgency. An emergency? I ran back down the hall, palette knife still clutched in my hand, and looked, slack-jawed, at the Ringers crouched around The Marshal's prone figure.

Unnoticed, I ran out of the room and into the larger of the two front bedrooms. I remembered seeing a white telephone on the chiffonier. I dialed 3166, the Rescue Squad number, and without even identifying myself told them to rush to Amber Trees for someone who had probably had a heart attack or stroke. This time the Ringers wouldn't get away with a cover-up.

Without warning, the receiver was jerked out of my hand. The voice eminating from the rancid body was frighteningly familiar.

"Who do you think you're calling?"

Turning around under his brutal grip I faced El Pricko.

"I'm calling my daughter, the Marshal's mother," I lied easily, "but she wasn't home."

His quizzical expression made me realize I wasn't wearing my wig, my steel rimmed glasses and my robe and probably didn't resemble the old granny he held in his arms Saturday night.

"I must go to Sonny. Excuse me young man."

I backed out of the circle of his vile smell and rushed back to the somber scene in the office.

No longer hunkered down around their leader, the men in the room were in conference, rather like a football huddle. They blocked my view of their leader's body.

One of the Ringers I recognized from the slide show moved from the group and came over to ask me a question. He wanted to know if I had seen anyone come into the office while I was painting.

I said no. "Will he be all right?"

The Ringer shook his head. "He's dead."

My heartless thought was that whoever had missed the last time had succeeded. The deceased had failed to touch any chord in my being. I was surprised at my complete lack of feeling.

Moving the portrait and easel into a corner of the room, I leaned against the wall. If my contributions helped to keep the Rescue Squad's reassuring beeper in shape I was glad. Soon the sound of it came through the windows. I could hear tires grind on the gravel road, doors slammed. Three saviors dashed into the room and knelt around the inert body. The rescue team was made up of two young men I didn't know and Wendy Holt, the press photographer.

As I watched them examining the body, Wendy rose to her feet and extended her arm displaying an object in her bloody hand. The trio grouped together and exchanged words.

"Where's the telephone?" she asked of anybody.

I motioned her to follow me. Two Ringers sprang to the door blocking our exit. Under my angry stare they changed their minds and moved aside.

Wendy dialed the State Police.

"I believe," she said into the phone, "the head man of the cult in Lofton has been deliberately killed. Yes," she said after a pause, "I guess I mean murdered." She walked to the bathroom and rinsed her hands.

"It makes me kind of sick. I think it was a pen-knife, it was slippery. Ted picked it up."

"Are you a nurse?" I asked.

She was a volunteer, but new at the job. "To find

161

a knife sticking out of someone's neck gives me the willies. But, I'd better get back."

The willies didn't cover my mixed feelings. "I'm going home now, Wendy. Please tell the police they can find me there."

"Oh, no, Mrs. McWhinny. The police said everyone should wait here 'til they come."

Seated on a hard chair, I waited half an hour for the police to arrive. After another half hour still more policemen brushed by me going into the office. Doc Smith came next, with his everpresent black satchel. He stopped.

"Tish, what are you doing here? Now I remember, you're painting his portrait. What did you do," he looked at my palette knife still covered with vermilion, "slice the fellow up?"

His heavy handed humor, I told my old friend, was not what I needed at the moment, but I asked him to please stop on the trip out and tell me what in the world had happened.

Lieutenant Lane introduced himself. Grateful to stand up, I shook hands with a compact dark-haired officer in uniform.

"I understand that you were painting a picture of the deceased." His brown eyes under heavy brows missed nothing on my face. "I admire anyone who can paint portraits."

The gracious amenities over, he steered me to a bench where we sat down.

Opening a note book to a fresh page, he said that the first procedure was to assemble all the facts. When, he wanted to know, had I arrived? How long had I worked? The time span he probed with the most precision was my trip to the sewing room.

Except for the time I arrived, every other answer

was a guess. It was impossible to be accurate about lapsed time when you're working. How long did I stay in the sewing room—seconds? Two minutes?

"Is that the only time you left the deceased alone in the room?"

"Yes. But," I pointed out, "he wasn't deceased at the time."

"We don't know that, Mrs. McWhinny."

Folding his pad, he slipped it in his pocket. He reminded me of my oculist as he moved within inches of my face.

"Do you own a Swiss army knife?"

My heart thumped and sent a surge of blood to my cheeks. Had I lost it in The Marshal's room? I rose above my irrational guilt to respond in a light tone, "Yes I do, Lieutenant. Doesn't everybody?"

He beckoned to a young officer who had been standing by the door. "Bring it over here, Chadwick."

"Does this knife belong to you, Mrs. McWhinny?" He displayed the bloody knife. Wrapped in the equally bloody plastic baggie it could have been a hot dog with ketchup. It could have had two blades or ten.

I denied ownership, saying my knife was at home.

With his eyelids at half mast and one eyebrow cocked, he listened to me babble on about different kinds of blades, imitation Swiss knives, old knives, new knives. When I ran out of steam, he rose to terminate our interview with the chilling news that Officer Chadwick would accompany me home and wait while I found my knife. That really made me angry.

"Is it your contention, Lieutenant, that I murdered that man?" I pointed towards The Marshal's office. "That I stuck a blade in his body then ran down the hall to the sewing room? It's preposterous". Trembling with indignation, I paused. "How was he killed?"

"With the awl, the ice pick sharp blade that opens in the center of the knife." He showed me the gory stiletto. Then, displaying his profile, he stabbed his index finger at the back of his head. "Here, just below the skull."

"He died in one minute?" Wouldn't he have caused a commotion, fought the murderer, called for help?"

"We'll know those answers eventually. You, Mrs. McWhinny, must know quite a lot about anatomy. But you're going to find your knife for us, aren't you?"

Doc Smith emerged from The Marshal's office with the same bustle and vigor that accompanied all his movements.

"Going to put her in jail, Captain?"

I didn't appreciate the jest. The Lieutenant didn't reply but led the doctor over to the window. I was dismissed.

Hilary stood with his hands on the gate's iron rods like a monkey in the zoo. He only let go when a guard opened them to let us pass.

"Good God, Tish, what's going on in there?" He took my arm. "I'll walk you home."

Officer Chadwick intervened. "Excuse me, sir. I have orders to walk the lady home."

"What in hell!" He still held my arm. "You can't ditch me, madam. I've been hanging outside these damn gates for hours. I knew there would be some kind of trouble today. You should have stayed home." He grumbled and complained during the entire walk.

Pete, at the garage with his wife, Lucy, Herb, standing outside the post office, and everyone who had been shopping at the store watched us proceed up the street. I waved to let them know I wasn't manacled. My shoulders were square, my head held high. I chattered brightly as though my police escort was a visiting nephew. It wasn't easy because panic does something strange to the back of the throat.

Hilary sat on the porch and Officer Chadwick, hands clasped behind his back, prowled around the living room. I tore the house apart in my frantic charade to the find the knife. Occasionally, I'd offer him feeble excuses or assurances that there were more places to look. Finally, with a show of empty hands, I had to admit that my Swiss army knife had disappeared. Or, as I added with a forced smile, "Maybe it's hiding someplace."

Or more probably, I thought grimly, it's in the palm of Lieutenant Lane's hand.

"Please tell the Lieutenant I'll notify him the moment I find my knife."

His body language spelled uncertainty. Should he haul me back to Amber Trees? Or did my gray hair, my frisky dog and my bright living room make me seem an improbable suspect? His youthful instincts won, but he did request that I make myself available for further questioning by staying at home.

18

No sooner had the Law left than Hilary came in to lay down his version of the Law. I was to compose myself in the wing chair, let him provide us with drinks to be followed by sustenance, then I was to disclose just what the hell this was all about.

"Lieutenant Lane suggests," I told him, "that I killed The Marshal with my Swiss army knife."

"And did you?"

"Don't be an ass, Hilary. This isn't a joke. Granted, I didn't especially like the man, but if I killed everyone I didn't like, my name would be a household word. Of course I didn't kill him. You know I can't even kill a mouse. But the point is what does the Lieutenant think?"

Hilary pressed my shoulders against the back of the chair.

"Tish, relax. Give yourself and me five minutes. You need nourishment."

As usual he was right, but relaxation was a state I felt sure was not to be in my immediate future.

During those moments, with comforting sounds emanating from the kitchen, I decided to tell Hilary everything. I had longed to discuss the bewildering and frightening events of the last few days, to hear his opinion about Lew and to force him beyond grouchy criticism into helpful thought.

His long brown hand put a glass of sherry beside me, along with a peanut butter and lettuce sandwich.

I drank my Tio Pepe with more haste that was appropriate for a drink that should be inhaled and savored. Its astringent elegance made me acutely aware of how close I might be to losing the worldly pleasures I took for granted. What were dimwitted pot smoking cultists doing in my life? How had my freedom become endangered by freaks who ate Twinkies and drank Mountain Dew? Could I be trapped by these dreadful people, by kidnappers and killers?

Ashamed of my sudden tears, I sobbed that it was all my own fault and threw myself on Hilary's compassion and wisdom.

"What will I do, Hil?"

"Start at the beginning. From the time you entered Amber Trees on Saturday afternoon."

But that wasn't the beginning. He scowled listening to my version of the first attempt on The Marshal's life. I dredged up every tiny detail of time spent in Amber Trees. I told him about Lew and that Kay and I agreed his name was Luke Welder. I gagged describing the bloody knife.

"What are we going to do?"

"We?" Hilary raised his eyebrows. He refrained from comment while he tamped the tobacco in his pipe. "We will start with your reporter. I'm used to calling him Lew. Why did he leave you in that hole, temple, chamber, whatever you call it? Was his plan to join the cult? Was he captured against his will? And why? Did he become a convert to the Ring of Right? A conversion to growing vegetables can't require much soul-searching. Now, turning in your favorite sport jacket for a gray night-shirt, that might be a little tougher."

"It's not funny, Hilary."

"I do respect your reporter, Tish, for the glimmer of common decency he displayed when he ordered you to get out of that horrible house. At least I assume that was your reporter. The unfathomable is why you ever went back?"

"We can talk about Lew all day," I said, "but until we talk to him, it's all conjecture."

"The police must be interrogating the Ringers right now," Hilary said. "Maybe Lew will come out of the closet."

I got up in disgust. "You're not taking this very seriously. Lieutenant Lane could be here any minute. Without a motive I'm sure they can't convict me of murder, but I can't and won't live under a shadow of suspicion."

Hilary stood up. "Sorry, you know I joke when I'm worried. And I am worried. Your situation is very serious. Circumstantial evidence has sent plenty of people to the gallows."

"Gee, thanks. You're such a comfort to me."

My determination was stiffened by Hilary's comment. I closed Lulu in the den. "Goodbye," I waved to Hilary from the door, "see you later."

He blocked my way. "Where do you think you're going?"

"There's no time to waste, Hil." I looked down the street. "We can make it. No police cars in sight. It's the perfect opportunity to inspect the farms. Everyone will be at Amber Trees."

"Forgive me, I'm dense. What do the farms have to do with the dreary druid's murder?"

"Don't you understand? If you don't want to bring

me brownies in jail, we've got to find out who did kill him."

"And you think the answer is at the farms?"

"Maybe," I said. "It certainly isn't at Amber Trees."

"You're crazy, Tish. Besides, I heard that cop tell you to stay home."

"Lofton's my home."

Usually I had to trot behind Hil's long stride, but cutting across the fields he had trouble keeping up to my jogger's pace. I couldn't blame my loyal friend for grumbling. Was I crazy? I knew it would be fatal to stop and analyze the possibility. What did The Marshal's disciples do twenty-four hours a day? I intended to find out.

Managing two greenhouses couldn't possible occupy twenty or thirty Ringers. Vegetable money divided twenty ways couldn't buy one tire for the mouse-ridden Porsche. Does marijuana pay that well? Were they bank robbers? The only way I knew to answer the questions that plagued me was sheer physical investigation with the wild hope that some object, a smell, a sound, a word would provide a clue.

When we stopped on the ridge I discussed strategy with my reluctant cohort. We decided to head into the valley to look at the greenhouses.

Their ugly plastic was mercifully hidden from the road, but we came upon them suddenly and had identical reactions.

"They're smaller than I expected," Hilary said and he read my mind when he added, "Could they grow enough marijuana in there to keep their fancy cars? How do we get inside?"

We skipped from tree to tree as though dodging a

fusillade of bullets and landed on our knees beside the end of the first greenhouse.

Hilary wasted no time prying up the plastic between the thick wooden stays. On all fours we looked underneath and had a good view of the newly cultivated earth. The only visible crop was so immature it appeared to be a green crayon line drawn on the dark soil.

Without fruit, flower or berries, it was impossible for me to identify a plant. Doug had been the gardener in our family. Fortunately, color, size and shape could be fixed in my pictorial mind until we consulted a horticultural dictionary.

Hilary slithered under the plastic. I held onto his trouser leg hating to lose him altogether. Pulling away, he crawled over to the virgin crop. His return was more difficult. I was terrified someone would hear his groans and curses as he wiggled his way under the foot-high opening. Opening his fist he dropped the green shoots in my hands. We both nibbled the oval leaves.

"Never tasted marijuana," Hilary said, "but this tastes like some kind of lettuce." I agreed.

Crouched like Peter Rabbit and the missus having dinner, we evaluated the situation.

After I talked Hilary out of bolting for home, I suggested we look in the cellar windows of the farm house.

If a Vermont farm house evokes a picture postcard image, dismiss it. This house, built into the side of a hill, was a triple split level carpenter's idea of a good living arrangement. The basement, which faced us, was the largest part of the house, the top levels were dinky by comparison. Unloved was a kind description of the dreary edifice and its untended grounds.

We crawled to within twenty feet of the back door.

"It's open." I poked Hilary. "You go around front and knock or ring the bell and babble to whomever is there and be sure to give me time to duck into the basement for a look."

"Field Commander McWhinny, I presume? You know, Tish, the second officer can take over if his superior is obviously insane. You are."

It's taxing to squabble in a whisper. Hilary's innate gallantry came to my rescue and he insisted that an insane female commander might be more effective as a distraction and that he would, against his better judgment, try to see what was in the basement.

We arranged a meeting place, five minutes hence, behind a thick stand of popple trees beside the road.

Seconds after I knocked, the door was opened by a pretty young black woman. At first I thought I had come to the wrong house. She looked more like a saleswoman from Bonwit's or Beneton than a Ringer.

"Can I help you?"

Hilary hoots when I describe myself as speechless, but her appearance completely disarmed me.

"May I please see Mr. Smith?" I figured that was a safe request. Even if she knew he was dead, I didn't see her as the type to conduct a seance.

"Alan Smith?"

"The leader of the Ring of Right. The Marshal."

"Oh," she stepped back, "you'd better come inside." She indicated I should sit on a green-stamps deacon's bench in the shabby entry. "How well did you know him?"

I sensed my grandmother ploy would be a big mistake.

"Did?" I raised my dirty hand to my mouth in

feigned distress. "Did you use the past tense? Did you say 'did'?"

"The Marshal is dead. He died." She pointed up towards the village. "He was murdered in his office."

"How awful," I exclaimed. "What happened?"

"No one seems to know for sure except some crazy old lady was painting his picture and they think she did it."

My lips formed an 'O'. It was one thing for Hilary to call me crazy, but to be characterized as crazy by this young thing made my dander rise. But only momentarily did I forget my mission.

"Why would this crazy lady murder him? Why wouldn't some of the inmates up there have more reason to kill him?"

"Ask the cops," she shrugged. "I hear the place is crawling with them." She appeared to remember I was an uninvited guest. "You can't stay here," she looked around her with apprehension. "Come on," she tugged at my shirt sleeve and ushered me out the door. "Hey," she had an appealing smile. "Don't tell 'em you heard about the murder from me. And please, lady, don't tell them you came inside the house, okay?"

"Okay." I tried to dawdle a little longer. She told me the correct time and I adjusted my wrist watch. I exhaled on my glasses and polished them on my shirt. I told her what a pleasure it was to meet her until I thought she might push me off the stoop.

I walked along the road. She yelled after me. "Where's your car?" I pointed toward Lofton and hurried out of sight.

What a lousy investigator you are, McWhinney. Who was this pretty young woman? A decoy for robbing a bank? I'd learned nothing except that she knew about Smith's murder and that her natural courtesy of inviting me in was against the rules.

Suddenly I had an escort on either side of me. Hilary looking frazzled on one side, and Walter Upson giving me a powerful and welcome lift on the other. Just off Main Street we paused in a maple grove.

"Want to know what I found in the basement?" Hilary asked. "I found Walter!"

"He scared me to death," Walter said.

"And just what were you doing in the basement?" I sounded sterner than I intended.

Both my companions looked stunning without their beards.

"Poking around, like Hilary. But we didn't have much luck, did we Hil? The place is a mess of gardening tools, fertilizers, markers, string, stakes."

"And shoe boxes," Hilary added, "lots of shoe boxes."

Walter corrected him. "Actually, sneaker boxes. Addidas, Pumas, Nikes. You name it, they've got it."

"What in the world would they do with all those sneakers?" I don't know what I had expected, but I felt disappointment.

"Empty boxes," Hilary said. "Maybe your boy friend had a shoe box fetish. Look." He handed me an Avia box. "There's something in it—powdery crystals—maybe it's cocaine."

Removing the top, I sniffed. The box smelled like new canvas shoes. I wasn't about to taste the white substance Hil described. We'd leave that to the police. The end surface said the missing foot gear was size six.

"Nothing mysterious about the box itself," I pronounced. "Probably they all bought sneakers at once at some discount place. Manchester's full of them.

The cleaning up was left to someone who can't throw boxes away. I have a little problem that way myself."

"Are you satisfied, Commander," Hil asked, "that an empty sneaker box and some Dr. Scholls' foot powder needed all that risk?"

The answer to that was probably no, but it was worth the risk to have found Walter. What did his presence at the farm mean? Was it the clue I'd been seeking? I asked myself the questions in silence.

Walter was disappointed when Hilary told him about the green buds we had sampled. He pulled a few mangled leaves out of his pockets handing them to Walter.

He sniffed and nibbled and reached our conclusion. "There's a lot of aerial surveillance now to spot marijuana crops. It's forced growers inside. I really expected to find it growing here. Vermont marijuana is supposed to be the best. Right now it brings two hundred dollars an ounce. I talked to a legislator the other day who was trying to figure out how to tax the state's second largest source of income. Did you look in the other greenhouse?"

"No," Hilary said, "and I don't intend to. How about you, Commander? I hope you're satisfied."

Satisfied was a poor word. I felt empty and confused. The will to follow a fruitless trail had evaporated. I related my unrewarding interview at the front of the house and admitted I was ready to go home.

"Prepare yourself, Tish," Hilary said, "the police may well be forming a receiving line on your front porch."

"Police?" Walter was stunned by the news of The Marshal's murder and indignant that I was implicated on what he described as silly circumstantial evidence. "I know Lieutenant Lane. Let me deal with him."

Hilary asked, "Are you going to tell the cops about seeing . . . ?"

I pinched his arm viciously and caught his eyes with a threatening look. If he was about to name Lew, he changed his sentence deftly substituting bland and meaningless words.

Walter seemed sufficiently occupied with his own thoughts not to have noticed Hilary's circumlocution.

None of us seemed inclined to small talk on the walk home. We were equally silent when we came onto Main Street and saw the group gathered around the front of my house.

19

"It's the press," Walter said.

"Couldn't be." I looked at my watch. It was two o'clock. He was murdered at noon.

"The Swallows' son works at CBS," I said. "If Birdie heard the news, I bet she called him."

Walter smiled. "This would be a first-class scoop."

"You mean 'Crazy Artist Murders Cultist Leader'?"

"No, silly. I mean 'Cult Leader Murdered in Vermont Village'."

"Stand tall, troops," Hilary ordered. "Let's go see what they want."

Half an hour later, Hilary and I were serving cider, cookies and sundry pantry goodies to a friendly group of amateur archeologists. They were members of Charlie Reed's Rock Club, his talk last week in Castleton having inspired their visit.

They took turns examining the rock that was still on the front porch. A young man said that Phoebe's Knee probably didn't mean anything, that it was obviously scrawled in a second. In fact, he said rubbing part of the inscription, one night in the rain and goodbye Phoebe's Knee. But the odd inscription was enough to rouse their curiosity.

The enthusiasm with which they described temples and chambers and solstice rocks was refreshing.

Their outdoorsy good looks almost made me forget the toads and monsters at Amber Trees.

I blessed Hilary for leading our visitors away. He suggested a search for Phoebe's Knee. The group followed him up the hill behind my house. I needed some rest and fell asleep in the den with Lulu curled up beside me. My dreams were about cheerful archeologists dancing and singing in a night club with Phoebe's Knee throbbing above them in neon.

My faith in Morpheus as a restorer of brain cells was not reinforced by my nap. Footsteps on the front porch wakened me to the same sense of ineptitude.

Lieutenant Lane's manner was courteous but solemn.

"We have reason to believe that Alan Smith may have been dead at the time the stiletto blade of your knife was pushed into the base of his skull, which accounts for the lack of blood at the scene."

I didn't let him finish what he was going to say.

"Thank God, that rules me out."

"But you didn't know he was dead, Mrs. McWhinney. You thought you killed him."

I jumped to my feet. Lulu reacted to my distress by trying to nip his ankle. Unperturbed he pushed her away. "Isn't that correct?"

"But the motive, Lieutenant, why would I kill anyone, much less a gross creature I barely knew?"

"We are told that you resented his presence in Lofton very much. We hear that the explosion in the root cellar was an incident that angered you, we hear . . ."

"This is utter nonsense, it's ridiculous. You don't kill people because they're unwelcome or irritating."

"Believe me, Madam, we don't want to upset you and we don't want to waste our time, but we will get to the bottom of this puzzle and we do regard you as a suspect. You have failed to explain the presence of your knife in Smith's office. We are not satisfied that any reasonably alert person could be in the room with a corpse for almost two hours and not know it. Particularly an artist trained to observe."

He held up his hand at my attempt to interrupt him. "And one of the members of the sect has informed us that you were seen inside their house Saturday night and not only were you trespassing, you were in disguise. If you would care to tell me about that event, please do so. If not, I will request a search warrant and we will no doubt find the wig described by our informant. Well, Mrs. Mc-Whinney?"

El Pricko had recognized me near the telephone. Damn. It would be impossible to fool this serious police officer, and what was the point? I vowed to leave Lew out of the picture as long as possible.

Characterizing my invasion of Amber Trees as a lark to satisfy friends' curiosity and my own about the Ringers, made me feel like a fool. It didn't help my ego either to see his look of disgust during my recitation.

He sighed and shook his head. I diverted his attention from my Saturday night caper by showing him the Avia box and its powdery contents. Hilary would be furious, but I blamed our trespassing there on him.

"How do these people support themselves, Lieutenant? Aren't the authorities interested in their activities? Is that cocaine in the box? Are they planning to grow marijuana? Did they rob the bank?" I thought of something I'd been meaning to ask. "Did you search Amber Trees?" He nodded. "Did you search the basement?"

He nodded again. "There is nothing there that would suggest they are breaking the law. We have been told that Smith was a clever and successful investor and acted as a broker for his people, many of whom pay to live there. He even gave them regular printouts of their stock market status. Guess it makes them feel good to make money and play farmer."

"They're an unappetizing lot," I said.

"I could agree with you there, Ma'am, but my personal opinion of the Ring of Right in no way alters the facts of Smith's murder. Someone killed him and I am not satisfied with the explanation you've given me about your presence there Saturday night. However, for now we must wait for the results of Smith's post-mortem examination. Perhaps tomorrow we will have more to say to each other." He frowned and leaned toward me as though he was watching his words sink into my skull.

With his hand on the doorknob he turned and delivered his last message. "If you aren't the murderer, Mrs. McWhinney, I suggest you ask a friend to stay with you. And lock your doors." He patted the Avia Box. "I'll take this with me."

Lulu looked at me quizzically as I talked to myself. "You're in over your head, old girl."

My admiration for Vermont's state troopers was enormous but I had to make my own way out of this mess. How could I sit back and relax the way the police and my friends, especially Hilary, wanted me to?

The archaeologists burst in while I was still trying to sort out my thoughts. Amusement crinkled the corners of Hilary's mouth. The club members were ecstatic.

"We found a solstice monolith!" A gray-haired

woman pushed a Polaroid picture of a pointed stone in front of me. "It's fourteen feet high. My God, it's beautiful. Now all we have to do is get behind that damn fence and find the chamber in its alignment. It's got to be there. He said," she pointed at Hilary, "that you knew how to get inside."

I shook my fist at grinning Hilary in mock anger. "Try the front gate. Today is a bad choice because, as Mr. Oates may have told you, the head honcho was murdered at noon."

When they left, Hilary was still beaming with pleasure. "Never had so much fun. It's all in knowing what to look for. I could have passed that Solstice stone a dozen times and just thought, 'that's a big rock'. It's leaning against a huge ash, it looks like part of the tree. They spotted it instantly. Can't wait to take you there." He took a closer look at me. "You okay? Did Lietenant Lane come?"

After I told him about our conversation, he asked me if I'd told Walker about the first attempt on Smith's life.

"No, I couldn't, Hil. I have this picture of Scarlett going down the stairs seconds after the attempt and damned if I'm going to implicate her. So maybe it's better left untold."

"Scarlett was at Amber Hills this morning," Hilary said. "I saw her walking around the back of the house a while before all hell broke loose. I saw Terry, too."

"Did you tell the cops?"

He shook his head. "I will, though, Tish, if the Lieutenant plays hard ball with you."

The picture of my phlegmatic model as a financial wizard fascinated Hilary. He laughed at my dismay that such people could be dancing to the Dow Jones. "You must think people who play the stock market are all yuppies or Yalies. Forget it. Money boys come in all sizes and shapes."

But regular financial reports, that is a laugh. What did he say, printouts? Guess they're pulled off a computer. I remember Kay describing that small room beside Smith's office.

El Pricko curled up studying the Standard and Poor 500 index was beyond the scope of my imagination.

"The police aren't going to solve this murder, Hilary. We have to. Here." I handed him my pen and a pad.

"What's this for? Shall I write down that Tish and Hilary are going to play detective? Haven't you had enough of that, or should I write: Tish wants Hilary to make an ass of himself raiding the lettuce beds in another greenhouse?"

"Oh, all right. Don't write anything down. But sit still and think. What do the Ringers do?" I didn't wait for his response. "If high finance is really their reason for being, why would they set up shop here in Lofton with all the home-spun and vegetable hocus-pocus? Dope is the only thing that makes any sense to me. It doesn't seem to be marijuana. Even though they smoke the stuff all the time, it must be cocaine."

"Lieutenant Lane should let you know soon about the crystals in that box," Hilary said, "but I guess I agree with you. Cocaine is the most popular, most profitable drug. It has to be distributed by someone. The Ringers drive in and out of Lofton all the time in limos and their super-charged cars. Amber Trees could be a major distribution center. And, of course The Marshal must be the financial genius."

"How do you deal with all that cash?" I asked. "The stock market doesn't deal in ten dollar bills."

"You launder it and what better place to do it than in a town with a big cash flow business like the Lofton Corporation."

"Oh, Hil, you don't think they're in on it?"

"Of course I don't, but how do I know?"

"That attractive black girl at the farm. I suppose she could be a front. That closet of city clothes," I remembered, "in the laundry at Amber Trees. They could be for the Ringers who have to look respectable selling to the fancy trade, like rock stars."

"Or," Hilary smiled, "selling to investment bankers. But, why kill Smith—the hand that guides them and passes out the loot?"

"Could be they're manufacturing the new version of cocaine—crack."

Crack, I had read, is processed into a purified form that can be smoked rather than sniffed or injected. Users are leery now of intravenous injections because of AIDS. Cocaine is much more potent in the rock-like form of crack, the article said it makes users instantly addicted and drives them to extraordinary lengths of depravity and lunacy.

"They could be cooking up crack right here in Lofton. It can't take much room. It's made in apartments in Brooklyn and the Bronx. The cover here is great. Who'd suspect a crop that usually comes from South America to be processed in Vermont? Maybe a couple of The Marshal's disciples were zonked out of their minds and for no reason at all wanted to kill the boss."

"How about Scarlett," Hilary asked, "What's her role?"

"With two teenage boys, it's inconceivable she'd have anything to do with pushing dope."

"Dealers distance themselves from pushers," Hilary said. "No one but scum works the school yards. The big shots are business men, but I agree, her involvement is impossible."

"She has a mystical connection to rock chambers," I said. "Druid temples and maybe feelings about Smith—guilt for bringing the Ringers here? I'm sure Terry is interested in his investment in the Inn, but kill for it? No."

The rock club people weren't very interested in Phoebe's Knee, but, as you heard, they're convinced there's a chamber to go with the solstice monolith."

"Let's forget Phoebe's Knee and Lew," I said. "We have to wait. We can't storm the gates and demand to see Lew. And the police won't help. Charlie Reed thinks Lew exists only in my balmy mind."

Lulu rejoiced when I got up to fetch her leash. "Walking makes the old bones work better, Hil. Want to join me?"

A hot bath was high on his list of important activities, he said, to be followed with a layer of soothing ointment on his briar-scratched hands. He then planned to take a nap.

From his car, he echoed Lieutenant Lane's warning.

"You really should stay home, Tish. I know you won't, but for heaven's sake, be watchful. These damn Ringers may be tame at Merrill Lynch but I don't trust any of them. You were there, honey, and since you didn't kill the man, maybe the murderer would like to know just what you did see. Think about it."

Hilary sounded so concerned I almost went back in the house, but I had an important mission in mind.

I thought of Walter Upson who had gone before

we identified Charlie's archeological friends. He had assured me he would talk to Lieutenant Lane. What would Walter say—that I was great fun, a very nice person and wouldn't murder anyone? What could anyone say—words weren't much help.

Kay had said that Walter often worked at home. I wanted to drop in and ask him a couple of questions. What was he doing at the farm this morning? Also gnawing at my subconscious was his remark at Hilary's dinner party about the Ringers leaving Lofton in the near future. The possibility of answers to those questions quickened my pace.

If Walter's pick-up wasn't in his driveway, I'd heed Hilary's advice and go home. The grassy parking space was empty, but I saw that the tiny square windows in the garage door were at eye level. I walked across the yard and pressed my nose against the glass. I wished I hadn't. The garage had space for two cars. The only car there was a pale blue Volvo.

20

Kay skidded to a stop in front of my house and brought me out of the trance that had enveloped me since my walk back from Walter's.

She jumped out of the car, displaying a mason jar. "Pesto! Made it today with the last of the basil. And," she handed me a brown bag of fresh green noodles, "something to go with it."

Before I could thank her she added, "And guess what I'm going to do right now? Pick up Walter and we're off to Boston for the Red Sox game plus some fancy wining and dining, and who knows what after that."

She had a beguiling leer. It disappeared when she said she hadn't seen me since the murder, but had decided that I should hire Lee Bailey to defend me, that I shouldn't take a chance of being railroaded by the Ringers or by the law.

I demurred, "Lee Bailey, dear girl, represents movie stars, oil moguls and zillion dollar corporations. Besides, I don't need him. I'm going to get to the bottom of this mess myself." I didn't tell her about finding Lew's car in Walter's garage, or that the sight of it had knocked me for a loop.

It was a depressing blow to think that Kay felt I needed the efforts of one of the nation's most prominent criminal lawyers. The story of the murder was becoming routine, but Kay wanted to hear every detail. I omitted the fact that Hilary had seen both Scarlett and Terry at Amber Trees.

"How about Terry," I asked. "Have you turned him in for a brawnier model or is he waiting in the wings?"

"Hey, what a question! I thought you were the big advocate of playing the field. Well look, Ma, I'm playing."

Her ebullient good spirits gave me a momentary lift but the dark silhouette of Walter stood somberly behind my smile. Was he in league with Lew—or with the Ringers? Was Kay in danger?

"Are you going to tell Walter," I asked, "about meeting Lew?"

"You mean Luke? No. Why would I do that?"

"It's fun to share a secret, and vino makes it easier," I patted her cheek, "but you're a strong character." Should I tell her about Walter so she could make her own judgment? I started to speak and stopped, I guess, with my mouth open.

"You have something on your mind, Tish. Out with it."

My mind, I explained, was addled, weary and worn. I was glad to see her leave, but hated myself for letting her go.

If Walter was connected to Lew in some way, he had lied to me and if confronted would probably have some glib explanation for the presence of Lew's car in his garage, and lie again. I decided to keep the disturbing discovery to myself.

No sooner had she left than a state trooper's car pulled up in front of me. Dreading another visit from Lieutenant Lane, I was overjoyed to see Charlie Reed's amiable face. He refused my offer of tea and stayed in the car to deliver a message from the Lieutenant. The substance found in the Avia box was a desiccant, Silicagel. "The stuff you find in little packages to absorb moisture. It broke and the crystals are what Mr. Oates found in the shoe box."

Hilary would be disappointed, finding cocaine would have enforced our convictions of dope peddling and perhaps have made the law take strong action about the Ring of Right.

Charlie nearly burst with excitement when I described his club's discovery of the solstice monolith. Only devotion to duty kept him in his car.

"Am I the only suspect, Charlie? Aren't they holding any of those hop-heads?" He shook his head. Through clenched teeth I told him that I knew, that my guts knew, that my instincts screamed that the Ringers were guilty of murdering their boss. That they were not benign farmers, they were criminals.

Charlie said that he would call me with any news of progress on the case, told me not to worry, and with heartwarming earnestness he warned me to be careful.

"Please, Mrs. McWhinney, don't do anything foolish, and stay home."

Why did everyone think home was so safe? Loftonites rarely locked their doors and my kitchen windows hadn't been shut all summer. If El Pricko were to lean against my back door, he'd fall onto the kitchen floor.

There was no more time to reflect on the lack of security of my house. Scarlett telephoned, primarily, she said, to tell me she thought it was terrible that anyone could even suggest that I killed Smith. Preposterous, was her word. Could she come to see me? She thought a discussion of events at Amber Trees was in order.

An indication of my spent condition was my complete inability to assemble my thoughts about Scarlett. I turned on the gas under my butter-yellow tea kettle and stared out the window. What an evil spell the Ringers had cast over Lofton. Suspicion and distrust could wreck our lives if, I could feel my jaw tightening, if we let it.

I'd seen Scarlett look tired before, but never drab. She seemed to have lost all her color. Perhaps her pink alabaster skin and pansy eyes needed to be lit from within. Even her hair failed to catch the light today.

She nervously lit a cigarette and inhaled to the bottom of her lungs. I had no pang of envy watching her smoke. It looked more like a necessity than a pleasure.

"I have a confession, Tish."

"Not for me, you don't. Try Father Casey or Lieutenant Lane." Maybe that sounded tough but I could almost feel the spring being pulled for a trap. I couldn't endure the burden of holding any more secrets. Confession is supposed to be good for the soul, but I was being selfish and thinking about my soul, not Scarlett's.

Undaunted by my lack of enthusiasm, she told me why the Ringers came to Lofton. It was a confession, she said, because she had begged them to come. She had promised to get them the best possible deal on Amber Trees and the farms. She didn't say so, but I suppose that her effort included discouraging other possible buyers.

Avoiding my eyes, Scarlett ran her finger around the rim of her cup. "I told you, Tish, that when I first met Alan Smith he seemed like a very nice man. I had dinner with him that evening we met. I think, unwittingly, I gave him the idea for this awful charade. We had breakfast together the next day and sealed the deal for the properties." The thought that she may have spent the night with Smith was repugnant to me.

"Exactly what do you mean, Scarlett, by this awful charade?"

"Smith led me to believe that he headed a syndicate of people who specialized in venture capital and other financial investments. He explained that privacy was of the utmost concern and that a country location would be ideal. To give the appearance of a harmless cult group was their aim.

"And," I peered over my glasses dismayed by the naivete of this practicing realtor, "and that's all you required in the way of a reference? Smith's say so?"

Scarlett paced the living room. "I'll never forgive myself, Tish, but the truth is I wanted to use them. My passion for the past, my heritage, my father, made me lose my usual sense of caution." I waited for her to build up a little more mileage on my oriental. "I feel sure there's an ancient Druid temple on Amber Trees' property but I've never been able to find it. Smith promised that it, or any rock formations or chambers, would be mine, or at least under my control."

I told her about the rock club's discovery of the standing stone. She raised her fists above her head. "I knew it, I knew it. How wonderful!" She softened instantly. "Then they blew up the temple that was partly on your property. I wanted to die. Instead of dying, I woke up and realized what a fool I was, that I'd been in a pawn in their despicable game.

"Smith told me the explosion was a mistake, but it was abundantly clear that he didn't give a darn about the explosion or about his agreement with me. I was shocked at the caliber of the people in the syndicate. I was mortified when I saw their costumes and heard and read the pretense about gardening. My talk about Druidic ways and customs must have given Smith the idea for their act."

"Couldn't you have protected whatever rock ruins there are without bringing in the Ringers to Lofton?" I asked.

She sat down again. "The notion of Celtic or Druid temples in Vermont is scoffed at by the state and therefore the law. Probably most people think it's archeological nonsense and the fabrication of kooky imaginations. I thought that if Amber Trees was bought by Philistines, it would be impossible to share our findings or even locate what I'm convinced exists. With Smith's cooperation I honestly believed we would all be winners."

It was my turn to pause. Scarlett looked sick when I told her I had seen her going downstairs right after The Marshal was almost electrocuted.

She put her forehead on her hand and sat that way while I poured more tea. This time I added an ounce of rum.

"The reason I wanted to die, Tish, is that on that particular morning I found out what Smith and his hirelings really do and I wanted to kill him. I didn't succeed. Thank God someone else did."

"What do they do?" I asked.

Clearly, Scarlett was going to tell it her own way. It took physical and mental fortitude to prevent me from bumming one of her cigarettes.

"Dope," she announced. "Cocaine." I closed my eyes while she lit up. After a swallow of tea, she rose and resumed her walk.

"Have you ever seen babies born of mothers who were using cocaine?" She told me about work she had done as a hospital aid before she came to Lofton. Her voice trembled when she described the horror of seeing blameless babies wracked with convulsions and inert tiny infants waiting to die. Her light voice graveled with passion when she described people in the black world of narcotics as detestable inhuman vultures.

"What happened that particular day?" I asked Scarlett when she recovered her composure.

"I saw your easel and canvas, Tish, when I walked into his office. I marched over and stood in front of him and said he was a liar and a cheat and worst of all, a dope peddler. He was blow-drying his toupee. He gestured at me with the silly little hair dryer. I don't know what he said. 'Don't bother me' or 'go away', but I slashed out at him and knocked the dryer out of his hand and it fell into his foot bath. I don't remember anything else except I ran out of there as fast as I could. Behind me I heard the sound he made, like the terminal bleat of a wild animal. I thought I had left the place unseen," she shrugged. "When I got home, I actually prayed. I remember saying, God, let him be dead."

She sat down, crying quietly. Lulu jumped in her lap to show the sympathy such creatures have for tears.

Hating to ask the next question, I examined my fingernails a while and recrossed my legs and finally said, "And on Saturday, Scarlett, where did you find my Swiss army knife?"

"Where did I find it? I've never seen your army knife. I wasn't anywhere near Smith the day he was killed."

"Hilary said," I took a deep breath, "that he saw you inside the gate of Amber Trees minutes before the murder."

That brought her to her feet again. Lulu decided I was more stable and jumped in my lap.

"I didn't go inside. Hilary may have seen me, but I was aiming for the back of the house. I had overheard a couple of Ringers talking at the gas station that morning when I was waiting to talk to Pete about snow tires. They didn't see me. Do you know about crack?" I nodded. She explained anyhow. "It's cocaine made more potent, and smokeable. I called a friend in Brattleboro who is a narcotics agent. He told me about crack. But he also said it was pointless to report the Ringers without any proof. He said he'd send someone up sometime. I couldn't wait for that, Tish."

"Did you find anything?"

She shook her head. "But I know it's there."

"You heard me at Hilary's dinner party. I've searched all of Amber Trees. Lieutenant Lane says the police have too, and they don't seem concerned. Where is the stuff?"

"Did you check the basement rooms?" she asked. I had to admit failure there.

"It's in the house, Tish. It's there someplace." She looked at her watch and said she had an appointment with a client. Again she castigated herself, accepting all the blame. I tried to comfort her while silently agreeing that she was a fool. She had done possibly irreparable damage to quite a few friends and strangers and to the town as well.

September's long afternoon shadows were melting into an early dusk. Like Mother Bear, I scrounged around in the kitchen to prepare food to sustain me through a long hibernation. I indulged my unlikely passion for tapioca. Stirring the milky potion slowly over a low flame soothed me. Eating the glistening fish eyes topped with pumpkin marmalade made me feel as relaxed as a sleepy baby. Mindlessly, I made my way to bed.

21

Lulu wakened me at seven. Thirteen hours was a lot to ask of such a tiny bladder. Old Morpheus had had time to work a little of his magic on both body and spirit.

A plan had come to my mind, one that might put an end to suspicions, doubt and accusations. Its only flaw, a grave one, was that it involved Hilary.

With the wiles of a gustatory mermaid, I lured him over for breakfast. French toast, he often stated, was my only touch of class in the kitchen. My secret was a very hot iron skillet, thick bread and a slice of orange to top the cholestrol-ridden marvel. I almost lost him when I described the clothes required for the occasion.

"Tame town clothes for breakfast? You're insane. What horrible scheme have you concocted in that twisted mind of yours?"

Sometimes Hilary was apt to show up in antique knickers and argyle socks, which wouldn't do today. Probably it was curiosity that made him come and, of course, the French toast.

I smiled at the thought of Lew's little brother gagging over his first encounter with French toast twenty years ago at the Inn.

The next half hour I spent at my drafting board creating an official-looking identification card. Was there a jail term in the offing for those who falsified documents? I doubted that a wallet-size card would be considered criminal.

We enjoyed breakfast before I told Hilary he was a health inspector. "It will be a cinch," I explained. "Walk right into Amber Trees and tell them you are making a regular inspection required for multiple dwellings serving food. But you know what to say, Hil. You have the gift of gab and you look sort of official."

I handed him a clipboard. The check list of violations had been fun to compile. Under 'Evidence of Rodents' I had typed: size? eye color? tail length? condition of teeth?

The questionnaire made him laugh, but he put it on the mantle.

"But why, Tish? Why, when you can't find anything, when we pulled a blank at the farm, when the police appear, at least for the moment, to be satisfied, why do you have to search further? Why me? What do you expect I'll find?"

I pushed him into the wing chair and tried to quote everything Scarlett had told me. "She knows the Ringers are cooking up crack somewhere. I don't want you to do anything, Hil, just look. Maybe you'll find a clue I've missed. When you come back, I'll call the FBI and tell them what Scarlett heard. I promise."

"You better mean that, Tish. Call them or Lieutenant Lane. The cops may not appreciate your interference."

"The heck with the police. It's time someone called the FBI or whoever handles narcotics. This one last time, Hil, one last look, please, for me. You don't want me to go to jail, do you? I thought we were going to be roomies at the Brattleboro Retreat?"

After I closed Lulu in the den, I put on my suede jacket and grabbed some Kleenex and my wallet. "Let's go", I said.

"And just where is it you're going? Could it be that you too, Madam, are a health inspector?"

"I'll wait for you outside the gate, Hil." I looked at my watch. "If you're not back in twenty minutes I'll come get you."

"Oh no, you won't. You'll go right to the phone outside the store and call Lieutenant Lane and tell him what a fool you've made of a faithful old friend. Promise, Tish, or it's all off."

I promised.

Pride swelled my bosom when I saw the alacrity with which an alert looking Ringer at the gate accepted Hilary's credentials. He beckoned another Ringer and told Hilary that Joe would accompany him on his inspection tour of Amber Trees.

Joe was built like a cigar box. He had a neanderthal hair line and a short fuzzy beard. His gesture indicating that Hilary should follow him was authoritative.

My view of the scene was from within a thick clump of spruce. I chose not to be seen by anybody.

At the end of twenty minutes I was frantic. My high spirits had descended to a new low. What had I done to Hilary? What kind of a rotten human being used her friends, her best friend? This wasn't like using your doctor's wife to get you into the Chilton Club. This was endangering a life, a very dear life.

Obeying the hands of my watch, I crept out of hiding and into the arms of the Ringer guarding the gate. With my upper arm in a painful grip, he pulled me along towards the porch. I yelled 'Help' at the top of my lungs hoping someone in Lofton would hear me, but the street in front of the store was deserted except for a Great Pyrenees who woofed in friendly response.

"Shut up." He slapped my face. The shocking experience was new to me and I shook with rising anger. Then he brutally thrust me through the door. Three Ringers blocked the hallway. Their faces were grim. Gerta, the object of El Pricko's lust, gave an order. "Put her down with him."

My voice returned and I complained ferociously as he dragged me down the hall. He didn't seem to feel it when I kicked his shins and beat on his arm. I tried to spit in his face, but couldn't muster up the saliva. Cretin, ape, misfit were among the names I yelled at him. Where was Lew? It was his turn to try to save me. I screamed his name—I fought all the way down the basement stairs.

"If you weren't an old lady I'd break your fuckin' neck."

He pounded on the door of the one room I hadn't seen, the door that had been opened a crack by the irritable Ringer in his undershirt.

When no one answered, he unlocked the door with a key fastened to his belt by a long chain. He pushed the small of my back and sent me crashing through the half-open door to land on my hands and knees on the rough concrete floor. The door slammed behind me.

Hilary knelt beside me. "It's alright, honey, get up." He led me over to a cot by the wall. Corduroy slacks had spared my knees, but the heels of both hands were painfully scraped. He watched me as I raised my head and looked around the room.

197

Anchored to the floor in the center of the space was a printing press. It was about the size of the love seat in my living room. I observed the stack of newly printed material beside the machine and raised my eyebrows. Hilary handed me a sheet which I read aloud. "The RIGHT way to grow vegetables" 'RIGHT' in caps.

I noticed the putty knife the printer had held in his hand. Hilary said it was for milling the ink which was done by squeezing it with the knife on a glass palette.

"Where's the printer?"

Without replying, Hilary walked around the press room touching things. As an old hand in the printing business, he must feel at home.

"That's quite a camera." He looked at a huge vertical copy camera. "And the guillotine looks brand new." He leaned over to examine the impressive cast iron cutter. "And a tip top contact frame. What a set-up."

Through with his tour, he straddled a wooden chair in front of me. "Are you ready for this?"

I dabbed at my hands with Kleenex. "From the beginning, please. I can't stand any more shocks."

Inspecting the house, he said, had been uneventful and fruitless. There were other Ringers about but no one spoke to him. He didn't see anyone who seemed spaced out or smell any marijuana or see any mice. The print room was the last on the tour. His guide ushered him inside. He described the printer as I remembered him—dark, thin and irascible looking. Cleaning his hands with a rag, the printer watched Hilary walk around the shop. He responded to questions in monosyllables.

Hilary murmured his appreciation when he ran his fingers over the top sheet of a pile of stock. Another stack of paper resembling parchment attracted his attention. He lifted a sheet up to scrutinize it under the strong ceiling light and let it fall back in slow motion.

"I didn't dare look at the printer, Tish. He'd quit cleaning his hands and was just standing there watching me. So was the other fellow."

Hilary got up and walked over to the cartons of stock in the corner and returned carrying a sheet in each hand.

"What's this?" He handed me one sheet. We both like good paper. I'd even made a couple of disastrous attempts to make my own water color paper.

"A high quality bond," I told him. "I can't guess the weight."

"That's right. Quality bond, about twenty pounds. And this?" He handed me the other sheet.

"A higher rag content, I think. And, of course, it has a color." Hilary handed me a loupe he'd picked up from the printer's work table. Flicking open what he called the printer's other eye, I pushed up my glasses and held the magnifier half an inch from my eye. "Yes, I'm right, a higher rag content. I can see the threads. So?" I sat back waiting for an explanation. Hilary isn't given to rhetorical questions.

He took the sheet back and tapped it with his finger.

"I saw those threads without the loupe. I kept staring at them because I knew what they meant. But eventually I had to raise my head. I had to look at the printer. Our eyes locked for a fraction of a second and he knew that I knew. He looked at the other fellow and nodded his head once and they both walked out of the room without saying a word and locked the door after them."

My expression was blank.

"What you are looking at here, dear lady, is a fine mezzotint of color and hairs, printed by an expert, printed on the white bond. It's a background for portraits of presidents, the most popular being Jackson, and for a picture of the White House. Funny money, honey. The heck with cocaine. They don't peddle dope, they're counterfeiters!"

Astonishment kept me silent for a few minutes.

"Where are the bills?"

"I've only been here five minutes longer than you have, but I haven't found any. They must have a pretty smooth operation moving the currency out of here the minute it comes off the press."

"Can a press that small make enough counterfeit money to run this whole shebang?"

Hilary tried to explain. "They have to cut one of these regular size sheets of paper into about 10 x 14. Then they cut out the water mark." He held up the white stock to the light so I could see the markings.

"How much could they make? Let's see." Hilary loved to juggle mathematic probabilities. "Four bills to a sheet. They have to go through the press a couple of times. Let's see. I'd guess eighty thousand bills an hour. At four dollars, which used to be the street price for twenties, that would be twenty thousand dollars an hour. T-men caught a counterfeiter a while ago who was fast asleep in a rattan chaise lounge while his press was spewing out perfect twenties."

"All the cutting—the trash must be a problem. You can't just cart bad runs of twenty or fifty dollar bills out to the dump. They must bring the stock here in those limos. After the bills are done, the Ringers must deliver them in that fleet of fancy cars.

"Counterfeit money plays a big role in dope transactions, probably plenty of it ends up in Colombia. But I think, Tish, all they need here is paper and ink, a press and a good printer—no imports."

He had lost my attention. I pulled the chair over to one of the windows to see if the fan in its metal frame was removable. It wasn't. It looked as if it had been cemented into the opening. This was also true of the window in a miserable little bathroom. Hilary was swearing at the remaining window which was covered with plywood.

"The damn screws won't budge. The grooves are too shallow. It's hopeless."

"Hey, I hear something." I turned off the fan in the window that faced the back yard. "They're yelling. There's some kind of ruckus."

The words were unintelligible. Hilary listened and agreed the tone and decibel level of the voices suggested anger, though he couldn't understand what was being said.

We found out soon enough. Three Ringers burst through the door. One of them, Hilary's hefty guard, held up his hands, his palms facing us. "Just shut up, do you hear me? Shut up and do as I say."

Neither of us is accustomed to being told to shut up. Hilary wasted a lot of eloquent vituperation to describe the trio's failings. I seemed to be in a rut, calling them cretins and misfits.

Our arms and hands were bound behind our backs with wide strips of masking tape. With my shoulders forced back, I thought my whole rib cage was going to be pulled apart. My words turned to groans as we were prodded like cattle out into the hallway and up the stairs.

The scene in the parking yard made my heart flood

with hope. Charlie was standing in front of his police car with a revolver held firmly in front of him.

Quite a few Ringers stood beside their cars. Two of them were loading a computer screen into the trunk of a Jaguar.

A Ringer still wearing her tunic carried a violin case to a waiting car. She looked straight at me and laughed. My bank bandit!

A group of about ten Ringers looked like campers waiting for a bus. Knapsacks and duffle bags were scattered. Only a few of the disciples wore their sackcloth robes. The feeling of arrested violence was palpable.

I made the first mistake. "Charlie," I called. "Help!"

From behind a Ringer produced an even wider roll of tape and brutally wound it around the back of my head and over my mouth. He added three layers while Hilary tried to bite him.

I'd been frightened before but never had felt such mortal terror, fearing that the tape so carelessly yanked around my head might cover my nose. The noises I made must have stayed his hand. I sank to my knees, vaguely conscious that Hilary was paying for his gallantry in the same terrifying fashion.

"So, Copper, put down your gun and walk over here or the lady gets it first." His gun jabbed me between the shoulder blades. "That will be when I count to five. The old gent will be next."

My glasses were askew and my eyes full of tears so that Charlie was just a blur.

22

Hilary tells me he thinks I fainted, I don't know. He says Charlie put his gun on the ground and walked toward us with his hands up. If there was a sigh of relief from anyone, it wasn't heard. The Ringers all scrambled for their cars. Charlie said later that the Ringers had been forbidden to leave Amber Trees since the murder yesterday and it was his job this morning to enforce the order. He said he was half asleep in his car when they all came tearing out of the building at once, obviously in a hurry.

The sound of engines roaring and tires skidding at the turn in the driveway even came through to me. The Ringers threatening us were the last to leave. First they bound Charlie's arms and made all three of us, me crying, stand with our backs to a skinny birch tree. They used two rolls of electrician's tape to fasten us to the trunk like rolls around a hot dog.

The three Ringers slapped palms and wished each other luck. Two of them jumped into a gray stretch limo and wheeled out of the parking lot. Sliding into a black Camarro, the last Ringer, with his gun still in evidence, darted out of the yard like a ferret.

Hilary nudged me as a dejected figure in street clothes emerged from the house. The Printer. He put two suitcases in a nondescript sedan and before he drove away looked at the back of the big house as though parting was a sad occasion for him. Was he taking samples of his work?

Hilary told me that buried in every printer's mind, even those free of larcenous tendencies, was the challenge of making a perfect twenty dollar bill. He was probably saying goodbye to equipment he loved and perhaps his home was wherever his press was bolted to the floor.

Charlie was frantically trying to free himself and succeeded in what seemed like an hour, probably four minutes. He tore the tape off Hilary's hands and ran to his car.

Sitting over the car phone, Charlie was able to tell Headquarters many of the Ringers' Cars' license numbers, which, thanks to his rigorous training, he had been able to memorize, along with descriptions of all of the Ringers' cars.

When Charlie came back, Hilary and I were sitting on the kitchen steps peeling tape off ourselves. We bemoaned the trials and tribulations of advancing age.

"I'm young, I'm strong," Charlie flexed his biceps in the classic gesture, "and what's more, I had a gun (now in its holster) and it didn't do me any good. I'll take you both home in a minute but I want to check out the house first." He stepped over us and took the rest of the steps in one stride.

Hilary was delivering a "what do you know . . . I'll be darned" soliloquy. I was literally licking my wounds. Wrestling out of the tape hadn't helped my hands.

We both stopped when Charlie returned, followed by a tall man.

"Lew." I wouldn't have believed I was capable of

jumping for joy. "You're safe. You don't know how glad I am to see you."

"Oates," Hilary stuck out his hand. "Heard a lot about you, young man. You look terrible."

A swollen cheek and bruised chin didn't interfere with the big toothy grin I remembered.

"You're one true friend, Mrs. McWhinney, but you scared the Bejesus out of me. I was sure you'd get killed. I guessed what you were up to when I heard that you were painting a portrait of the Marshal."

"You've restored my sanity. Most people,"—I didn't look at Charlie or Hilary—"thought I'd taken leave of my senses and that you were a phantom. How did you . . . ?"

"Not now," Charlie said. "Let's go. You two coming or do you want to wait for us here?"

Before I could ask where they were going, Lew said, "Phoebe's Knee, you know, I told you about it when we took our fall."

A reply was impossible. By this time we were jogging through the woods. Had he told me about Phoebe's Knee and perhaps the fall had dented my memory? Questions would have to wait.

A new lightness filled my body. The breezy feeling in my head was worry blowing away. Euphoria cushioned my feet as we leaned into the steep hill.

Skirting an arrangement of boulders and fallen trees, Lew turned and grinned at us. He leaned down and picked up a balsa-light tree trunk moving it to one side. On his knees, Lew ran his hand over gray rocks shaped like an inverted V.

"These rocks must have fallen against the cave opening hundreds of years ago. See? Her upper leg is this bulge and down here, doesn't that look like a paw," he beamed at me, "like your dog's paw?"

It took a little imagination, but that was my long suit. Lew said he wished his brother Fred was here. "We found this place when Grandma's dog, Phoebe, vanished inside."

Charlie couldn't stand one more word or gesture that kept him waiting outside. On all fours he disappeared under Phoebe's knee.

The last to enter the dark cavern, I could just barely see the built-up walls and the huge slabs of rock overhead.

"A chamber," Charlie crooned, "a real chamber." He echoed our thoughts when he cursed himself for not bringing a flashlight.

"Here it is." There was no mistaking the elation in Lew's voice. "Here's the proof. Look, Officer. Box after box of it."

He crawled by me with a shoe box under his arm and we all followed him outside.

Leaning against Phoebe's Knee Lew passed around twenty dollar bills. We rubbed them, folded them, crinkled them. Hilary smelled his. It took me back to childhood parties where we gambled with paper money.

Charlie was more excited about the discovery of Phoebe's Knee than he was about playing a stellar role in the bust of a vast counterfeit ring. It wasn't until we'd wrenched ourselves out of the spell cast by the perfect ersatz bills that we realized he was missing. Hilary had to crawl back under Phoebe's Knee and pull him out of the mysterious ancient structure.

Bemused, we walked for a while in silence.

Lew remarked on the fence. "It wasn't here when I came."

Charlie told him that it had been installed after the dynamiting of the chamber we fell into.

"The Marshal chewed the boys out for that one," Lew said.

Talking was impossible while we walked single file and Charlie and Lew had to give in to our request to save questions until we reached my house. I didn't want to miss a word they said and when we got home there was even a larger audience.

The Ringers' mass evacuation had left the villagers in a cheerful state of puzzlement. Terry, who saw us from the Inn as we left Amber Trees, followed us home. Kay and Walter drove up to the door about the same time we did.

I make the rules in my house, and I issued orders that not a word was to be spoken until those starring in the drama had a chance to go to the bathroom. My hands needed attention and I could tell Lew was grateful for the chance to wash his bruised face.

I introduced him properly, as Luke Wedder. "I'm a spy," he smiled, "like Mrs. McWhinney. And what happened to my face? Well, I guess when Mr. Oates here recognized the background stock for the bills, he blew the whistle on the counterfeiting operation. The guys must have decided they couldn't knock off both you and me too. I didn't wait around to find out. I made a run for it, but my least favorite giant thug caught me and bounced me off the wall until he decided he'd better leave with his chums. I was surfacing when your officer found me."

"From the beginning, Lew, Luke," I begged. "Start way back when we fell in the hole."

"The chamber," Charlie solemnly corrected me.

"I was about to pull you out of there when I heard these guys talking and figured it was the Ringers and that it would be better to sit tight. They were so close they practically fell in with us. I almost had to strangle your dog to keep her from tearing after them. I told you I was going up to Phoebe's Knee, but now that I think of it, you were pretty woozy."

"You told me about Phoebe's Knee?"

"You kept saying spell it, so I scratched it on the rock beside you. Then Lulu escaped and figuring that help would come, I ducked into the shrubbery—didn't want them to find me. Thought when you saw the film I stuffed in your pocket you'd catch on."

"Catch on to what?"

"That I was all right. Though I suppose I was a little rattled myself. I remember thinking I should quickly shoot off the last couple of exposures to get the film out of the camera. The paper expects pictures from me daily and I figured since I intended to head for the mountain, it would be safer with you. How was the picture of the Ringers' feet?"

"You photographed part of a robe," Hilary said.

"How did they know Tish had the film?"

"The can must have rolled out of my case. Or they may have just been guessing. As you said, Mrs. McWhinney, they're extremely camera shy."

"For a good reason," Kay said. "What a story! When will your book be out?"

"Two weeks after I start it." I could tell she liked his grin, too.

"So," he smiled at me, "I waited until the ambulance people came, scared silly they would find me. While I was waiting in the bushes there I got the idea of infiltrating the sect, but figured I'd go up the mountain and do some heavy thinking first. Ask him," he pointed at Walter. "We met on the mountain and got talking and I told him what I wanted to do. He encouraged me and said he'd help by taking my car, and if I changed my mind, just to come and get it."

"I told Luke here," Walter said, "that if he could get those pot-heads out of town I'd be a big backer of that newspaper he wants to start." He beamed at Hilary. "How about that land, old boy? I promise, no condos, just ski trails. Honest."

"We'll see," Hilary said, which, when I was a little girl, meant probably not, but his expression was beatific.

"Thank you, Walter," I said sarcastically, "for your help when I tried to find Lew when I got back from the hospital. You're a good liar."

"I try," he beamed. Kay told us to shush.

"It was exciting to find Phoebe's Knee, just as I remembered it." Lew paused to explain to the others how he and his brother and his grandmother's dog had found the chamber. "Inside, I could tell by the atmosphere that the place had been used in some way. Then I found a twenty dollar bill and out in the light I saw the green ink had smudged and the numerals weren't sharp. And that made me decide to take the plunge.

"The Ringers bit, hook, line and sinker," he went on. "I showed up at the basement door, said I'd lost my knapsack and was out of work and let it be known I was a printer." He answered Hilary's raised eyebrows, "Worked in the union press in Brattleboro one summer. The Marshal interviewed me and assigned me a buddy who never left my side, except when I was locked in the press room, which was most of the time, or put to bed on the third floor with a guard at the door."

"Who killed Fatso?" Kay asked.

"What a great name for him," he smiled. "I hope

Fatso died of cardiac arrest before he got skewered by the awl. I think it was two of the Ringers. The Marshal was hell on coke. Any of the brethren who used it got the worst punishment of all—no money, funny or otherwise. He didn't mind marijuana, but this new crack! These two guys were horrors at best and often boasted they were going to knock off the boss. My buddy figured them for the job. I guess they tried to pin it on you, Mrs. McWhinney?"

I smiled and nodded like the Queen Mother. I'd never felt so relieved and happy in my life. I asked Luke if the Ringers had robbed the bank.

"Someone robbed a bank. The boss was wild. Wherever it was, it was too close to home. For those guys a bank heist comes under the heading of recreation."

Kay told him about the storm of real currency at the Londonderry bank and asked, "All that business about the stock market, was that a front?"

"Probably not. It was another way of manipulating money. Your friend Fatso loved playing the market and he had to scratch hard to keep them busy, They showed gangster movies on VCR every night and other instructive films, like the one you saw," he looked at me, "that told the men to leave anything that looked like a rock chamber strictly alone. And there was a film designed to teach them the difference between a turnip and a beet, with a reminder that manure was called manure. They were a pretty tough bunch of cookies and used to a lot of action. Smith had to let them feel like big shots, but keep them in line. Quite a trick."

"Were the wigs and beards part of the Druid hocus-pocus?" Kay asked.

"Yup, and how my buddy hated it. He'd rather be

wearing alligator pumps and a thousand dollar suit, but Smith ruled with an iron fist. They went berserk when he died. Self-government obviously wasn't among the courses any of them took in Sing Sing."

When Luke stopped to attend to the drink he'd earned, Walter wondered aloud what would happen to Amber Trees and the farms now that Smith was dead.

"Stink was his name." We all looked at Terry. "Smith's real name was Stink." Blasé about surprises, we sat in silence. "And my name isn't Fink, it's Stink—or used to be."

Trying to control wild hysteria, I urged him to continue.

"It mortifies me to tell you, Tish, to tell all of you, but you'll find out what I found out last week, that Alan Smith, The Marshal, and I were cousins."

Our various reactions made us sound like geese and gobblers. I had to admire Terry's control as he quieted us and went on to tell us that Stink was a name that made his young life miserable, and that both he and Alan Smith had changed their names years ago.

"He was my father's brother's only son and I was an only child. So," Terry gave the word a long reading, "my lawyer tells me that maybe, just maybe, if Uncle Sam doesn't put the place on the dock, that I might, just might, inherit the house."

We cheered.

"My uncle lived in Scranton. I only saw him and Alan when we were little kids. All I knew was that he'd changed his name to Smith and was a big shot in some kind of shady business. Wasn't until I saw him at the explosion that it all came together. Scarlett had told me he was from Pennsylvania. Suddenly

211

there he was, standing there looking just like my uncle." Terry had our undivided attention.

"Scarlett had repeated to me the conversation she overheard about manufacturing crack at Amber Trees, so I thought a little honest blackmail might be in order. I planned to threaten him with exposure unless he slowly but surely packed up and left town. Scarlett guaranteed she'd sell the place for him. Well, you know what happened. Never even talked to him, and he left feet first."

Engrossed by his tale, the room was quiet for a minute. Then Kay asked, "What will you do with that huge house, Terry? Another inn?"

"We've already thought of that. Oh, I know, counting chickens and all that, but Marty and I thought we'd run a cooking school inn and we'd grow vegetables at the farms."

"A great idea," Hilary said. "Let's raise our glasses to our distinguished neighbor. Lofton will welcome more of your tax dollars, young fellow. Here's good luck to you." We all drank to that.

Charlie, who had been standing by the door while we listened to Luke and Terry, said he had to leave. I knew he could hardly contain himself in his eagerness to get back to Phoebe's Knee with proper light. "They'll catch those people," he assured us.

"Just don't bring them back to Lofton," Walter said. We all expressed similar sentiments.

"We won't be chasing them, Mr. Upson. With all that evidence, the Treasury men will do the job. The Lieutenant will want to see you right away, Wedder. I'll see you Saturday, Mrs. McWhinney."

"Saturday?"

"The rock club is meeting here in Lofton. Wait 'til they hear about Phoebe's Knee. We'll be wanting to line up the standing stone with the entrance of Phoebe's Knee."

Lulu curled up in my lap while Luke answered questions.

The shoe boxes to hold the counterfeit currency, he said, had taken the place of cigar boxes, which had traditionally been used since the eighteen hundreds when counterfeiting was at its height. "We never had bills in the press room for more than an hour after they were finished. I'll say that for Smith, he was a whiz at organization. Lofton was the perfect place for his business, a difficult area for surveillance and good for swift distribution by private cars. They probably had a network all over New England. The bucolic facade really worked."

"About the printer? You must have gotten to know him?" Hilary asked.

"Not really. Personally, I think he was a prisoner, imprisoned by his own dedication to perfection. He lived for his work. He could have been operating in the basement of the White House for all he cared. Smith must have had something on him. Who knows? That cousin of yours was a really smart operator," he smiled at Terry, who winced.

"Lay off, please, and let's keep this quiet—except for Scarlett. She's been sick with guilt. I'm going to find her now. Think we'll have to make her Town Manager of Druid Temples."

He turned at the open door. "Just think, we'll be able to print our own menus."

"What a book!" Kay had moved over to the couch beside Luke. "And the movie!" She leaned toward him and put her hand on his arm. "We won't have to sign up Meryl Streep for my part. I'll play it myself."

23

Thanks to the drink Hilary had put in my hand before Luke started to talk, I was suddenly anesthetized. Alcohol, the time of day and the morning's trauma had made retirement imperative. I was enveloped by oblivion the minute I collapsed on the bed.

Two hours later, feeling refreshed, I brushed my hair and contemplated with pleasure the thought of a cup of tea, perhaps a tea with authority, like Irish Breakfast. Once again, I could walk into my studio with an unfurrowed brow, enjoy the familiar props and glory in the lovely light. Maybe Hilary and I, all of us, could eat at the Inn tonight and laugh about the tyranny of the Ring of Right.

From the stairway, I saw Kay's red car still parked in front of the house. In the kitchen, I noted glasses and plates in the sink. Probably Hilary had provided lunch for Kay and Walter and Luke after I went upstairs.

I was just about to pour my tea when the phone rang. It was Charlie Reed. He wanted to talk to Luke.

Kay walked into the kitchen.

"Just a minute, Charlie." I held the receiver to my chest. "Is Luke with you? Charlie wants him."

She shook her head.

I smiled when Charlie said he wanted to discuss

Phoebe's Knee with Luke. I looked at Kay when I put down the phone.

"Something the matter?"

She shrugged. "Sorry about the dishes."

"Forget the dishes. What's on your mind?"

She sat in the chair opposite me and poured herself some tea. Folding her arms, she leaned her head back. "When you went upstairs," she said, talking to the ceiling, "Hilary left and suddenly the euphoria evaporated. Walter decided we needed some coffee. I made sandwiches—we talked. You risked your life for Luke. We thought you should know."

"Know what? Please don't tilt that chair. Look at me, Kay. What are you trying to say?"

Lulu barked when Luke knocked on the door. He came in and picked up the wriggling creature. "Kay hasn't anything to tell you, Mrs. McWhinney, I have."

"Tish, please."

"Tish. I haven't been straight with you."

I pulled out the chair beside me. Kay took Lulu and let her out the back door. She stayed by the door gazing up at the clouds on Lofty.

Looking at Luke, I was surprised I had missed his drawn expression. He rubbed his long hands together as though he was trying to erase the swirls and patterns on his finger tips.

"That day we met in front of the store. I knew about the Ringers. I knew about Smith."

I suppose my eyebrows had moved up an inch, but I said nothing.

"Walter told me about them."

"Walter!" My eyebrows had a little farther to go. "From the beginning please, Luke. My ability to comprehend is at a low ebb."

He examined his palms for a moment. "Teddy died more than a year ago."

"Your brother?" I asked. Luke nodded. "I'm sorry. Do you want to tell me about it?"

"Teddy died of AIDS. The doctors feel sure the virus came from contaminated needles. He wasn't a Haitian," he said bitterly, "and he wasn't a homosexual. He was a drug addict. He was addicted to cocaine. Dying took six awful months."

"I've heard that intravenous drug use is regarded as a much more important factor in the spread of AIDS than had been realized. Were you with him all the time?"

He nodded again. "I quit work. He was an incurable optimist, so cheerful, right to the end."

Lulu had run around the house and escorted Walter when he announced himself and came in through the screen door.

"I heard you talking, Luke." Responding to my gesture, he pulled out a chair. "Tish, what you don't know is that Teddy was the greatest guy in the world and my best friend. I didn't know about the dope. I didn't even know he was sick. I was working in Australia and hadn't seen Teddy for about a year. In fact, I never saw him again."

"Walter came to Teddy's service at the college chapel."

"What has your brother's death got to do with Smith and the Ringers?" I was perplexed.

His brother, Luke said, was unable to resist get-rich-quick schemes and often was involved in hairbrained enterprises.

Walter's smile was rueful. "That was his specialty at school. I don't recall any successes, just catastrophes."

"The ultimate catastrophe," Luke said, "was when he fell in with Smith on a money scam. I never did find out just what it was, but Smith must have pushed Teddy into something criminal."

"For all his bravado," Walter said, "Ted was a nervous Nelly, and Luke and I think he used cocaine as an escape from guilt or anguish."

"But," I interrupted, "you told me Smith didn't tolerate people who took drugs."

"Only if they worked for him. I have a feeling," Luke said, "that it suited Smith to see Teddy fall apart. More than anything, I wanted an answer to those questions. Teddy refused to tell me anything about his work or his past escapades. I was determined to ask Smith."

"I'm the one, Tish," Walter said, "who told Luke that Smith was here in Lofton. Smith sort of vanished after Teddy died. It took me a couple of weeks to realize that our head Ringer was the Alan Smith that Luke had described. We concocted a scheme."

"And you fell into it, Mrs.—Tish. You changed the course of events. Your determination to find me warmed my heart but it made my blood run cold. Thank the Lord you're here and all in one piece."

"Did you ask Smith about your brother?"

"Yes. I gave my buddy the slip and confronted Smith that morning. I saw your knife on the floor. I didn't know it was yours, but I picked it up and fiddled with it when I talked to him. When I told him my brother was Teddy Wedder—"

"Wedder?" Kay asked. "How come Smith didn't recognize your name when you first met him?"

"I'd told him my last name was Weston. He knew who Teddy was all right, but he barely looked at me. He kept on reading some damn stock market report.

I tore the paper out of his hands and shouted at him. "What happened?" I kept asking him. "What happened with Teddy?"

"Finally he looked at me. He said Teddy was a jerk and got what he deserved, or something like that. He leaned over to pick up the paper and in a rage I swung at him. He spun around in a full circle and the awl on your knife, which I had in my fist, drove into the base of his skull."

"I'll bet he twirled around," Kay said, "because he was having a heart attack."

"Let's hope so," Walter said.

"I know what they mean about adrenalin adding a rush of strength. Lifting his inert body back into the chair was almost impossible. I didn't touch the knife. I placed his hands on the chair arms, put the paper over his head and ducked out just as I heard your voice, Tish. Now I'll never know what happened to Teddy."

I put my hand on his arm. "There's no reason to believe that anything an insensitive thug like Smith had to say about your brother would be illuminating. Have you told Lieutenant Lane?"

"Do you think Luke should tell the Lieutenant, Tish?"

Kay moved behind my chair. "Not a fair question, Walter. Tish, as unreasonable as it seems, is still the number one suspect. It was her knife. She was there. Of course she'd like to get off the hook."

"Partially true, Kay. But I can't believe the Lieutenant thinks I killed Smith. The physical mechanics of the deed are too unlikely and of course I have no motive. Don't tell the police, Luke. In your anger you probably didn't even realize you had the knife in your hand. Tell the Lieutenant what you told us about the two drugged Ringers killing Smith. I believed it, maybe he will."

"That's just what I have been telling Lane and your friend Reed, Tish. I don't know if they bought it."

"They will, Luke. You did us all a favor. Just think there's one less rotten person in the world. Smith was a killer. There are two kinds of people in this world—killers and lovers."

"And an assortment of dead-heads," Walter added.

"Takers and givers," Kay suggested.

"Same thing. Sounds milder, but they're just as devastating. Let's rejoice! We're all lovers and so was Teddy. Think how happy he'd be, Luke, that you found Phoebe's Knee safe and unspoiled. That reminds me. Officer Reed wants you to call him at Amber Trees." I flipped through my phone number wheel and dialed the number, handing the phone to Luke.

It was lovely to see his big grin when he put down the telephone. "The doctor says Smith died of cardiac arrest."

Kay hugged all of us and Walter kept saying Hurrah, hurrah. You'd think the deceased had won a race.

"Why," I wondered out loud, "hadn't Charlie told me about the autopsy results when he called a few minutes ago?"

"He just found out himself," Luke said. "He was telling me about the markings he'd found on the portal of Phoebe's Knee when he was handed the autopsy report."

I said, "Hurrah to you, Doc," to myself. Had Doc acted as a citizen of Lofton glad to be rid of the leader of the cancerous Ring of Right? Had he pre-ferred Smith's name to appear on a roster of coronary fatalities instead of stating that his death was caused by a lethal weapon which, of course, would force the law to produce a murderer? If so, "Hurrah for you, Doc."

"Kay," I handed her the phone. "Call up the Inn and see if the boys can raid a flotilla of lobster pots. I think Lofton has something to celebrate tonight. My party."

"Will do. I hope you're paying in new twenty dollar bills, Tish."

Luke stood up and pried a roll of bills out of his pants pocket. "Let me, Tish."

Why, you crook." Kay held out her hand for the bills. "Are they counterfeit?"

Luke grinned. "I don't know. I kept a couple of twenties to compare with ones I had, and now I can't tell them apart."

"We'll let Hilary smell them at dinner." I looked at my watch just long enough for my friends to take the hint. "See you at seven."

From the front porch I waved goodbye to the lovers.